G000088658

Dragons

are a

Girl's

Best Friend

Quarter Witch Chronicles, Book 1

JOYNELL SCHULTZ

JOYNELL SCHULTZ

Copyright © 2019 Joynell Schultz
All rights reserved.

ISBN (print): 9781097146086

WET DOG PRESS

Cover by www.coveraffairs.com

DRAGONS ARE A GIRL'S BEST FRIEND

On the outside, Ruby's a normal college student.

On the inside?
She's something else completely.

Magic runs through her veins, tempting her to use it, but Ruby isn't sure how to control her new powers...until Ty, a dangerously handsome man from another world, spots her and identifies her as a witch. He offers some answers, but they come with a cost.

Not only does using her powers make her a target to others trying to steal her magic and slay her pet dragon, but each act of magic must be balanced—and **magic takes whatever it wants.**

Is all the chaos caused by casting a few spells to ruin her ex-boyfriend's perfect skin worth it?

Heck yeah.

Learn more about the *Quarter Witch Chronicles* on Amazon HERE.

Series contains three books:
Dragons are a Girl's Best Friend
While the Dragon's Away
A Good Dragon is Hard to Find

JOYNELL SCHULTZ

Table of Contents

Chapter 1

"I don't think you should sell the house." Geoff tossed his long brown bangs off his forehead and plopped down on one of the few pieces of furniture remaining in the Victorian home I grew up in.

"Sure, now you say something." I crossed my arms over the giant pi sign on my t-shirt and playfully narrowed my eyes at him and shrugged. "You're too late. Besides, what's an eighteen-year-old going to do with a house, much less this monstrosity?"

"It just seems like a shame."

"If only one of us had an extra thousand dollars a month lying around to help me cover bills. I don't have much of a choice. You and I are moving to Bloomington later today, and there's no way I can pay both the bills and my college tuition." I dropped down onto the sofa next to my boyfriend of three years.

Geoff wrapped a thick arm around my shoulders and twisted strands of my long, amber-colored hair around his fingers. "Didn't your mom leave you some money?"

"Sure, but I have college to pay for." Especially out-of-state tuition, but I didn't say that. Going to Indiana for college was ultimately my decision—even if it appeared that I was only following Geoff's lead.

Two men from the Salvation Army stumbled down the stairs, carrying an old oak desk from my mom's office. As I watched the piece of furniture being taken away so carelessly, memories of sitting on my mom's lap at that desk while she balanced the checkbook flooded my head. She'd give me a piece of her fancy stationery to scribble on while she crunched her numbers. My heart ached with emotions I thought I had finally gotten a grip on since she died four months ago.

"Ruby, are you crying again?"

I wiped my eyes, snuggling into Geoff's side while he guided my head onto his shoulder. I don't know how I could have gotten through the past four months without Geoff. He was something stable in my life. We dated for almost our entire time in high school, and during the past year or so, when my semi-normal life dissolved into something I no longer recognized, Geoff was beside me every step of the way. I had lost my mom, moved out of the only home I knew, and was in the process of going away to college.

Oh, and did I mention I discovered I was a witch?

Not really a witch, I guess. I was mostly mortal, but still had one-quarter magic blood which was still unique because powers were a thing of books and movies, not real life. The man who supposedly was madly in love with my mom nearly nineteen years ago was half witch, but he took off, disappeared into thin air right after Mom told him she was pregnant with me.

Mom always showed me the bright side of her situation: that she got me out of the deal, but as I grew older, I realized she had been hung up on my biological father for the rest of her life. She never got married, but had a live-in boyfriend for most of my childhood until that fizzled out when he finally asked her to marry him. She said she never stopped loving Dad.

What was all that passion like?

Sure, I loved Geoff—at least we said we loved each other—but I couldn't imagine forgiving him if he took off on me, leaving me to raise a child by myself. Mom was just that compassionate.

I wiped my tears again, snuggled deeper into Geoff's side. "I'm sorry. I'm just missing Mom right now." Even though Geoff gave me sympathy, he didn't know what it was like to not have parents. With my absent father, it had always been Mom and me…up until she died of breast cancer. Since then, it was like a huge part of me was gone. "Actually, I miss her all the time."

Another Salvation Army volunteer came down the steps, carrying an old chair that sat in the corner of my mom's bedroom.

"You're getting rid of the green chair?" Geoff pulled away from me, letting me sit alone on the cold sofa. "That chair is awesome! I want it."

Geoff had already collected dozens of things from my house after Mom died. There was no way all that stuff would fit into his dorm, but who was I to stop him? I was giving it all away, anyway. "Take it. I hated that eyesore." But as I watched some oil paintings, a bookshelf, and a bedframe go out the door, small parts of my heart went out with each piece. "Maybe we should go somewhere else." Somewhere that I didn't have a view of the front door.

A noise came from upstairs, and as I turned, I caught a glimpse of one of Mom's paintings fall out of a volunteer's hands and tumble down the stairs along with a glass mirror. The edge of the painting frame hit the railing of the stairs, taking a chip out of the finish, and when the mirror shattered against the painting's delicate canvas and the picture turned over, giving me a glimpse of Mom's favorite painting—the one that hung right over her bed—my heart nearly leapt out of my chest.

"No!"

The painting of the elephant balancing on a beach ball fell in slow motion with glass shattering all around it. The animal tumbled feet over head down the steps, as the glass scraped the picture.

It was being destroyed. Mom's favorite painting was being destroyed. It'd soon be gone, just like her. My breaths were heavy and my vision threatened to go black. I couldn't breathe. I needed to calm myself. I wasn't the only one in the world to lose a parent.

Without thinking, I dug my hand into my jean's pocket, fisting the silver medallion that Mom gave me from my dad. A faint static charge tickled my skin, and I pulled at the magical electricity like it was something tangible. The piece of silver was all I had that proved to me that I was a quarter witch. It was also the only thing I had from my father. Why had my mom kept it a secret until a few days before she died?

Magic prickled my skin, crawled up my arm, and filled my core with power and confidence. I focused the power towards the painting to stop it from rolling down the stairs and being destroyed further.

And like most times I tried magic, it didn't work.

Heck, I only got magic to work a few times before, and if it weren't for those instances, I'd never have believed my mom's last delusions. There was no magic in the world. I had spent hours and hours searching the internet for anything on magic and witches, but was left with nothing substantial, yet I know the medallion was an object that helped me do magic—sometimes.

The painting fell off the bottom stair and laid face up

with a big rip down the center of the elephant.

"That's enough!" I sprang to my feet, surprised at the emotion in my voice. I wasn't ready for this. Four months wasn't enough time to heal. From the kitchen, the two men who had the dresser were now carrying out the kitchen table, and I completely lost it. "Stop! That's enough. We're done." The volunteers looked clueless.

"Leave the table. Leave everything. I'll call you back when we have a buyer for the house." Which wouldn't be long, the real estate agent assured me. Apparently, the market was hot for big Victorian homes in this neighborhood due to the community college nearby. Why hadn't I chosen to go there?

That answer was easy. It was because Geoff was going to the college out-of-state, and I didn't want us to separate. Considering the circumstance with my mom, I couldn't take being alone right now, and I couldn't afford the house.

"But the truck's only half full." The head volunteer readjusted his dirty baseball cap. "At least let us get the piano out of here for you." He pointed to the upright piano in front of the picture window.

I shot him a don't-mess-with-me look, and he backed down, rounding up his coworkers and heading outside. I locked the door behind him.

"What was that?" Geoff sat down in his new green chair, rubbing his hands down the wooden armrests.

I swallowed my thoughts. "Nothing. I just thought we should have some furniture here until the house sells." It was a lie. A complete lie, and I didn't mind telling it.

Geoff shrugged, his hair falling over one eye. "Let's get going then. We have to make the trip to our dorms."

I knelt and picked the glass away from Mom's painting,

pulling the canvas off the frame and carefully rolling it up. Could it be fixed with tape? Sure, it was just a print and I could order a new one, but this was the one my mom's hands had touched.

My legs were heavy as I tried to stand and follow Geoff out of the house. A little scrape in the hardwood floors drew my eyes. I accidentally scratched it when I tried to sneak a TV up to my bedroom one night. More memories rushed back to where Mom hung a coat rack on the wall, but missed the beam and left a hole in the drywall. Of where thick, ugly yellow curtains once hung that we picked out together. Of the stain on the carpet that I swore was caused by my imaginary friend for years until I grew up and realized there were no such things as dragons. Sorry, Luke. The memories were too much, and my chest constricted.

When Geoff left the house, I cast my eyes to the ground and followed along. It was best that I sold the house. I didn't need to be haunted by memories of Mom, though I tucked the print tightly under my arm. I wasn't giving this one up.

I was an adult, and many adults lost their parents. They all functioned just fine.

What was wrong with me?

It was time I grew up.

I was going off to college.

I was starting a new life.

And I was going to learn how to use my magic.

Chapter 2

In my dorm, I sat cross legged on my twin mattress with my mom's torn painting and the medallion from my father in front of me. Could my magic repair this painting? It was a long shot, but two weeks had passed since my emotional meltdown at my old house, and maybe if I fixed the painting, I'd be ready to move on. I'd be able to return the calls to the Salvation Army and schedule a time for them to take the rest of Mom's things away.

College started tomorrow, and I wanted to begin my adult life with a clean slate which involved closing one chapter of my life and opening another.

I picked up the tarnished silver medallion between two fingers and held it up to the single overhead light, smiling at the goofy dragon on the face of the coin.

When Mom first told me about my dad's lineage, I promptly voiced her words to Geoff. We both had laughed that Mom had been given too much morphine.

When she gave me the medallion and made me promise to always keep it on me, a few strange things happened.

Coincidences, maybe.

Like at my high school graduation, when I turned the medallion in my hands while silently wishing the class valedictorian—who had tormented me about my MIA father for my entire life—broke one of her four-inch-heels while walking across the stage. The little piece of silver made my skin buzz from a static charge, like when I placed my tongue across both ends of a 9-volt battery, and just like that, it happened. The girl I avoided my whole life tumbled onto the

13

ground.

Occurrences like this made me believe what Mom had told me about my father, as crazy as it sounded.

If only she was alive for me to ask more questions. I traced the index finger of my free hand along the tear in the canvas painting, silently promising myself I'd fix it for her.

Being a quarter witch meant my powers were erratic. Sometimes they'd work, but most times, they wouldn't.

And they weren't very strong—not that I knew how strong a witch's powers could be.

Mom had said that Dad could do magic. He could make a cat talk—not that they were very intelligent—and light up a room with a wave of a hand, but said this world wasn't meant for magic and he couldn't do it often. Right before he left her, he made her promise to tell me about my abilities when I was an adult, but with a warning that it would come with consequence.

Sounded like some B-rated movie.

Maybe he couldn't do much magic because he was only a half witch, but I wondered what he meant about consequences? Would magic turn me evil? Would it take the life of someone I loved? Or was it something else completely?

I held the half-dollar sized piece of silver in the palm of my hand and traced my other finger along the coin's ridges. The symbol on the face of the coin was fitting, since my childhood imaginary friend was a dragon.

I hadn't figured out anything about my magic. Could I practice it and make it work consistently? Figure out what triggered it to work? I was scientifically minded, and wanted to know if there was some secret I needed to discover, or would it always be nothing but a few random occurrences.

As I ran a finger of my free hand along the cut in the painting, wishing it would mend, nothing happened.

I closed my eyes, pointing to the start of the rip, and squeezed the medallion in the other hand, wishing, hoping, needing it would mend.

For Mom.

For my memories of Mom.

The silver warmed in my hand, and my heart skipped a beat. I opened an eye, but the painting was as broken as it had been. I refocused on the silver and the painting, thinking of how the picture looked over Mom's headboard and remembering crawling into bed at night with her while she read me a story. I'd stare at the painting sometimes more than the picture books, thinking about her words, "Anything is possible."

Even an elephant balancing on a beach ball.

The warmth of the silver faded, and my eyes opened to a perfectly mended painting.

I did it!

Mid-yawn—since using magic seemed to suck my energy away—I jumped at a knock at the door.

"Who is it?" I threw my legs off the bed and stubbed my toe on my desk.

After living in a three-story home for my entire life, my little one-hundred and fifty square foot dorm room felt like I was in a cardboard box. There were bigger rooms here at Einstein Hall, but that would mean I'd have to share with a roommate. Paying a bit extra for a private room gave me the freedom of Geoff staying over—if he wasn't caught.

I had suggested we move in together for college in a couple's apartment, but Geoff thought we should live the typical college life during our first year.

Perhaps that was for the best. It gave me time to myself to practice a bit of magic—which I hadn't told anyone about. I needed to be able to consistently use my abilities so nobody (aka Geoff) didn't think I was crazy.

"Who else comes to visit you?" Geoff called through my room's old wooden door.

I unlocked the deadbolt and was greeted by my boyfriend's wide smile, but there was something off about it. It wasn't as big as normal.

"I didn't expect you." I stepped aside so he could sit on my desk chair while I sat on my bed, pushing the mended painting aside. I finally had the proof I needed to confess to Geoff that I was a quarter witch. I sucked in my bottom lip, holding back my smile. It would finally be great to tell someone about this. I had kept magic to myself for months, and the secret was starting to eat at me. I wanted someone to share my excitement. To help me work on my magic. Maybe even find out if there were more witches out there...

And I trusted Geoff. He wouldn't call me crazy if I had proof, and even if he did think I was crazy, he'd stick by me. I knew he would. He loved me.

And I loved him.

Geoff folded his hands on his lap and sat up straight, tossing his messy bangs off his forehead. "I came over to talk."

My heart sank at his seriousness, and I tilted my chin. That was odd. He usually came over to fool around. Again, a good reason for the private room.

"Sure. We can talk." I tucked my legs underneath me on the bed. I reached over and rolled up the painting. My confession would have to wait. "What's up?"

"Are you nervous about tomorrow?" he asked.

"A little." Was this what he needed to talk about? His hand rubbed against his jeans like he did when he waited for the dentist or when he was giving a speech at school. I added, "I keep telling myself it's no different than high school. Just a different building. We go to class, study, do homework, and take tests. Nothing new."

Geoff nodded, not seeming to pay attention to my words. He took a deep breath. "I'm just going to rip the Band-Aid off and do this quickly." His eyebrows knitted together, then his face went blank—distant. "I think we should break up."

I froze.

What did he just say?

Surely not that we should break up?

We just were talking about when we would get married last week, though both of us decided our teenage years were too young.

But we were committed to each other.

Weren't we?

I searched his face for any sign of what he was thinking, but he had looked away from me. His lips pressed tightly together, and his hands fiddled with his jeans.

My lungs lost their air, and I felt like I was at my mom's funeral again, with all her coworkers and my classmates and teachers giving me a hug and wishing me their condolences.

But they didn't know how I felt.

I had thought Geoff did…

He glanced back at me for only a moment before looking down at his fumbling hands. "I thought we should break up during our senior year, but then your mom got sick." Someone must have punched me in the gut, because I felt like vomiting.

He was really breaking up with me.

After everything we had been through?

And was he telling me that the only reason we stayed together was because my mom was dying?

How could he even tell me that?

Did he not have any compassion at all?

He was talking, but I didn't want to hear the ridiculously long list of reasons. Tears were threatening my eyes, but I grabbed on to my anger instead of sadness.

"Why didn't you tell me sooner? Like before I moved all the way here to Bloomington?" I tightened my lips, waiting for the answer.

"You've been so sad. I thought a change of scenery would be good for you." His voice grew quiet.

"Because you know what's best for me?" My anger was bubbling up from deep inside. "And now I'm here in Bloomington with nobody. At least back in Arcola I had Sonja." My thoughts were becoming incoherent. "Just go." My arm jetted towards the door. I wouldn't let him see me cry.

"Ruby, I still want to be friends. I just thought we should live the college experience. I want to go to parties and meet new people. I want to date other girls before I decide to spend my life with one in particular. Maybe we will still be together in the future, but I need a little bit of freedom. I want to—"

"Stop! Go. Leave." I opened the door and pointed into the hallway. I needed space. I needed air. I needed time to think.

Geoff hung his head low as he headed out into the hallway. I expected him to stop and apologize for what he just done.

But that didn't happen.

Instead, he hiked away, moving faster and faster the further he got from me.

How long had he not loved me?

How long did he suffer while staying at my side?

Since my mom got sick? That was nearly a year ago when she was diagnosed with cancer.

He had led me on for nearly a year?

And using the excuse he knew what was best for me? What a load of BS.

Once my door was closed and the deadbolt engaged, I let the tears come.

Three years of my life thrown away. Given to him with nothing more than a quick goodbye.

I sank onto my bed and stared at the crack in the ceiling plaster. I couldn't believe he said that maybe we'd still get together? After you break up, that's it. I wasn't the kind to wait around for a guy. I wasn't going to be like Mom.

If Geoff wanted to live the college experience, good for him. I'd give him that experience and show him that two could play at that game.

And I'd have more fun doing it.

I was the one with magic.

And I was glad he didn't know.

Chapter 3

The next morning, I popped out of bed and pushed all thoughts of yesterday out of my mind. This was my first day of college, and I wouldn't let some stupid boy get me down. I had been pathetic. Who cries all night over a teenage romance, anyway?

Surely not me.

I showered and dressed in my most broken-in jeans and favorite periodic table t-shirt. I needed to be comfortable for a full day of learning. I pulled my deep amber hair back into a ponytail, and I was ready. Thousands of people went to school at Bloomington University, all I had to do was avoid Geoff, and I'd be fine. When I pulled my schedule out to map my classes, I realized that thought was an impossibility.

I had my first class with Geoff. I scanned through the rest of the day, remembering when we compared schedules. I also had the last class of the day with him. We had done that on purpose. No, not *we*, but rather, I had worked to line up our schedules.

Now I realized how idiotic I had been. Geoff was going to school for business, and while I wasn't quite sure what I wanted to do when I "grew up," I knew it was in the science or math fields. Why did I try to get classes with Geoff? There was no reason to even run into each other during a day at school, but we coordinated it twice.

I cringed.

No problem. I could get through this minor setback. When I toured the college, I remembered the giant lecture halls. I still might be able to avoid him.

That bubble was crushed the moment I walked into the economics lecture hall, and Geoff was right behind me.

"Hi Ruby," he said, like nothing was wrong.

Two could play at that game.

"Morning, Geoff." I flashed a smile, but when my eyes tingled from the threat of tears, I veered to the left, taking a spot about a third of the way back in the lecture hall. I heard footsteps behind me. Geoff must be following.

Was he having second thoughts?

I wouldn't give him the satisfaction of a glance. Willing my tears away, I wiggled into a seat midway down the row, and the person who had been following settled behind me.

The room filled slowly. My mother always instructed me to be early. She'd say, if you're fifteen minutes early, you're on time, on time was late, and late was not an impression you wanted to leave.

So, I always shot for fifteen minutes ahead of schedule.

As I watched the other students filter in, I realized how different this truly was from high school. These were not kids. Some students were old enough to be my mom, others were definitely in their twenties. The boys had full beards, and the girls were…well, women. I felt like a child.

A familiar head toss, the one Geoff did to move his bangs out of his eyes, caught my attention from the other side of the lecture hall.

He hadn't followed me. I twisted to see a girl with thick-rimmed glasses in the row behind me. She smiled, and I returned the gesture before focusing back on Geoff.

What was he doing way over there? He scooted into an aisle directly between two girls—and not even a chair apart, but sandwiched between them. The red-head laughed and flipped her hair off her shoulder. The brunette reached over and wrote something in Geoff's notebook.

My pencil broke in my hand—and it wasn't from magic.

Maybe I wasn't over him.

I turned to the front of the room, focusing on a grey-haired man futzing with some electronic equipment laying across a table...and the sight from the shadows beneath it made me look twice.

I rubbed my eyes and blinked. In the corner of the stage, tucked deeply under the slab table surface, red, glowing eyes stared out into the audience.

My body tensed. After over thirteen years, I'd recognize those loving eyes anywhere—they were from Luke, my childhood imaginary friend.

My dragon had come back. My heart pounded. I had been crushed when Luke seemed to disappear into thin air so many years ago, but it had coincided with me going to kindergarten and my life changing—not to mention my realization that having an imaginary friend was not normal.

Maybe my life changes were triggering him now?

Or was I going crazy?

What adult saw a dragon who was invisible to everyone else?

I swallowed a lump in my throat.

I had thought my father had schizophrenia, and that's what the whole magic talk was about.

Maybe I did too?

Had I repaired Mom's painting, or was that just in my head?

I stared beneath the table, but the eyes faded.

I could handle this. I knew I could.

"Is this seat taken?" a male voice asked.

I snapped my head up to see a thin, athletic student with light brown hair and hazel eyes. He flashed me a charming, slightly crooked tooth smile. I glanced around him to catch Geoff's stare from across the room.

I straightened in my seat and pulled out my best, sweet smile. "No. Have a seat. I was hoping I wouldn't sit alone." A bit of the truth. A bit flirty—if I even remembered what it was like to flirt.

Was it too soon?

Yup, you bet.

Did I care? Not at all.

"I'm Ruby." I reached out.

"Liam." He took my hand in a firm handshake that made a warm tingle spread through my stomach. Maybe being single would be fun.

Maybe Geoff had been right.

Liam sat down and pulled out a notebook. "First day?" he asked.

"Is it that obvious?" I tucked a wisp of hair that had escaped my ponytail behind my ear, thumbing the paper in my notebook resting in my lap.

"Here." Liam reached over me, giving me a whiff of citrus, and pulled out a little table tucked beside my seat. It dropped over my lap and formed a writing table. "The chairs dub as a desk for taking notes."

My cheeks heated. "You must think I'm an idiot."

"No. Just a freshman." He smiled. "Besides, any girl who wears a periodic table of the elements shirt on the first day of class couldn't be an idiot." He winked and turned towards the front where the professor tapped a microphone. I searched for the red eyes of my dragon, but they were gone.

"What year are you in?" I asked.

"Junior."

"And you're in econ 101?"

"I changed my major and still have lots of time before graduation." Liam sat back in his chair.

The girl behind me whispered into the back of my head. "I hear this class is boring."

"I wish I would have known," I whispered back.

"Tomorrow, I'll bring a cup of coffee."

"Mmm, coffee. I hear that University Grounds is good and reasonable," she said.

Liam twisted in his seat. "How about we meet there tomorrow, an hour before class?" He flashed that charming smile.

The professor's voice suddenly drowned ours out, and I nodded, as did the girl behind me. "My name's Kat," she whispered.

I twisted over my shoulder. "Ruby."

Perhaps this college thing would be alright. Day one and I already seemed to have made two friends.

One was exceptionally good looking—and a bit older than me. I guessed about twenty or so. And a nerdy girl who made me feel right at home.

I couldn't wait to see what the rest of the week brought.

Chapter 4

As usual, I arrived fifteen minutes early to University Grounds Coffee Haus the next morning. My new friends, Liam and Kat, weren't there yet, but someone else was.

Geoff.

I clenched my jaw as I maneuvered through the crowd to stand in line to order a mocha. With full whip today. I needed the smooth comfort that only high-fat dairy could bring.

Out of the corner of my eye, I watched Geoff interact with the redhead he sat next to yesterday morning in economics. He leaned his elbows on the table, and she laid her hand on top of his and giggled.

Wow, he moved fast.

After ordering, I scooted to a corner of the coffee shop as far away from Geoff as possible, but I still had a visual. I should have sat with my back to him, but I had to watch. It was like driving past an accident where you couldn't help but look.

What was Geoff doing here with her?

Had they been dating before Geoff broke up with me?

With as comfortable as they seemed together, I wasn't ruling that out.

And why did I care? I didn't want Geoff back. With as much as he crushed my heart, there was no repairing it, but the spiteful side of me wanted to see one hint that he had cared about me. I wanted reassurance I hadn't thrown away those three years with him.

Geoff scooted around the table to plop down on a small sofa bench directly next to the girl. She leaned down and whispered something in his ear. He brushed her hair away, but instead of whispering something back, he kissed her! Right on the lips.

My heart leapt into my throat.

Sure, it was closed mouthed, but still, we *just* broke up.

"Ruby?" the barista called. I jumped, turning away from Geoff. Why had I watched that? I'd be better off not knowing. I took my mocha and sat back down with my back to my ex this time.

Maybe I'd get over it.

As I sat there with my mocha cooling, all I could think about was if that redhead, with designer clothes and too-much eyeliner would have even given Geoff a second glance if she had met him as a pimply faced, scrawny sophomore like I did.

I took a sip of my coffee to calm my nerves, but then, the weight of the medallion in my pocket called my name.

I reached in my jeans and pulled out the silver coin.

Hmm.

If that redhead knew Geoff when he had red bumps on his face, would she still be kissing his cheek?

The medallion warmed in my hand.

Oh, a bit of magic couldn't hurt.

I wished Geoff's perfect skin goodbye.

It wouldn't work, anyway. My magic, if it really did exist and I wasn't hallucinating it all, was so sporadic, but the thought gave me satisfaction. I lifted my mocha to my lips, needing a heavy dose of caffeine. I wish I would have slept better the last few nights; there was nothing like starting a day exhausted.

"There you are."

I stood up, flipping the coin into my hand and shoving

it into my pocket. "Liam. I didn't see you come in. How long have you been here?"

He dismissed me with a wave of his hand. "Ahh, don't worry. I just got here. I haven't even ordered yet."

"I haven't seen Kat, either."

Liam ran a hand through his short hair. "She's not coming. I had the last class of my day with her yesterday, and she decided she wanted to sleep in rather than wake up so early."

I laughed, thinking how pathetic it would have been if Geoff was here with a date and I had been all alone. "Well, I'm glad you came."

He smiled, showing off a slightly crooked eye tooth. "I'm glad I came, too. Wanna stand with me in line while I order?" He nodded towards the counter.

"I'd love to." The thought of sitting alone at this table any longer made me cringe. I glanced over my shoulder to see the redhead running her finger down Geoff's perfectly smooth cheek. Yup. My magic was useless.

I fought back a yawn, realizing I really needed the caffeine this morning. I picked up my coffee and followed Liam to the front, giving Geoff a scowl as I passed. I noticed Geoff's eyes on me…or rather on Liam. Hmm. Let him think what he wanted. I stepped closer to Liam to prove a point. "Are you an early riser?"

Liam turned towards me. "I don't sleep much. You know—college life and all. I'm not a morning person necessarily. More of an opportunistic sleeper."

I laughed. It wasn't that funny, but I wanted Geoff to see me moving on without him. I glanced back. He hadn't noticed.

"Who is he?" Liam asked.

I snapped my head back towards the tall, handsome man in front of me. "Who's who?"

He nodded towards Geoff. "Him. You keep looking his way."

My cheeks heated. This didn't look good. Maybe it was time to come clean. "My ex. Recent ex, I guess. Maybe it's too soon to be here with you." I laughed, realizing what I just said. "I mean—it's not like we're on a date or anything. I just should be locked in my room mending my heart after being dumped the day before starting college after a three-year relationship." I shrugged, willing myself to not spill my life story. "Did I say too much?"

Liam held his thumb and index finger up, showing me an inch of air between them. "Yeah. You may have said a bit too much." He glanced over my shoulders at where Geoff sat. "It looks like he moved on quickly, huh?"

"I'm still trying to decide if he was cheating on me. We moved here three weeks ago, and it's not like we spent every moment together. In fact, he had been distant—"

"What does it matter?"

True. That knowledge would only make me angrier.

"Wanna do something fun?" Liam moved forward with the line.

"I don't know. I'm having a ton of fun already," I teased.

"Well, I thought we could make him jealous." His eyes were fixed behind me to where Geoff sat. "When he glances your way, I'm going to kiss you."

I choked on my saliva. "What?" I had only been kissed by one boy in my life, and he sat behind me, nuzzled against another woman's side. I had only had one boyfriend, unless you counted the little pretend fling I had in seventh grade where we got as far as texting each other a few times. Before I could agree—or argue—Liam's lips were on mine. His strong arms wrapped my torso and pulled me close. Where Geoff's kiss was sloppy, Liam's was precise and calculating. Before I could contemplate more, Liam pulled away, and stepped up to the counter and ordered his coffee like nothing had happened. With a pounding heart, I couldn't help but spin around to see Geoff's face.

All I got was an angry glare.

I smiled and shrugged.

He moved on.

And so did I.

And I was sticking to that story.

Chapter 5

Liam walked me to class, telling me all about this underage club he discovered this past weekend, not even mentioning the kiss.

I tried to listen to what he was saying…good music…dancing…specialty alcohol free cocktails and snacks…yada yada yada, but my mind hung on what his lips felt like on mine—warm and an odd combination of soft and hard, if that was even possible.

What did Geoff think?

Who cared what Geoff thought? What did I think?

I wasn't quite sure.

Liam escorted me down the steps of the lecture hall, and we shuffled into nearly the same seats as yesterday. Kat wasn't there yet. I couldn't help a quick glance to my right—over two sets of rows to where Geoff had sat yesterday—and our eyes met.

I quickly cast mine down, but not before noticing a red blotch on his cheek.

I looked back, not caring that he saw me looking at him, and realized I hadn't seen a red blotch, I had seen a cluster of red blotches.

His perfect skin was gone.

OMG.

I hexed him.

Served him right.

Liam nudged my shoulder. "Stop looking at him. You'll make him think that you're not over him yet."

Which was true, but I formed a smile. "Sorry. Old

habits." I shrugged and sat down in my seat, adjusting the little desk across my lap and relishing in the fact that I had done a bit of magic—even if it wasn't quite the *right* thing to do. After pulling out my notebook and pens, I heard someone take a seat behind me. I twisted to see Kat. "Hey, I missed you this morning," I said.

She leaned forward and pushed up her glasses. "You did? Liam said it was okay if I skipped, that we'd get together tonight at Young Monsters."

"Young Monsters?" I looked to Liam.

"It's the underage club I was telling you about."

I connected the dots. Welcome to college, Ruby. Liam coordinated a private date with me this morning and then coordinated a private date with Kat for this evening. That two-timer.

But we hadn't been on a date. I would have believed that, except that he kissed me. A kiss meant nothing, right? We were adults now, in college and dating casually.

"Sounds like fun," I managed to mumble before microphone static filled the auditorium speakers.

"Good. You should come along," Liam suggested. "I was trying to ask you on the way over, but I got carried away with my long-winded explanation."

The ice in my heart melted. Maybe he wasn't trying to date us both, but maybe he wasn't trying to date either of us. "Sure. Sounds like fun. What time?"

"Good morning, ladies and gentlemen," came the professor's voice.

Liam whispered, "Seven."

I didn't know where Young Monsters was, but I could look that up. I nodded and turned towards the front of the room.

Halfway through class, an open door on the side of the lecture hall caught my attention. Actually, it wasn't the door that got me, it was the glowing red eyes in the darkness beyond. Luke the Dragon was back. I focused on him as the professor's monotone voice filled my head, talking about the elements of a market economy and scarcity.

Was I crazy, or was Luke really there?

Crazy, right?

But then, who believed in magic?

Luke stuck his head out, his long, golden nose first, followed by his eyes. They no longer glowed out of the shadows.

I searched the lecture hall. Was anyone else staring his way?

All eyes were on the professor or taking notes. I was imagining Luke. The dragon looked up the rows of seats to the back, fixated on something for a moment, then jetted himself into the closet.

Something crashed inside.

The room jumped, and my heart sped up.

Maybe he wasn't imaginary.

And if he wasn't imaginary, why had he returned after thirteen years.

And where did he come from?

I spun around to see what had startled Luke and caught a glimpse of a man leaving the doorway.

Was Luke hiding from someone?

Did he need my help?

"Settle down," the professor said as he walked to the closet. He flipped the light on inside, and there, in the back, cowered Luke. The professor, and the entire two-hundred-some kids in the lecture hall, didn't seem to notice the golden dragon about the size of a border collie. The professor picked up a metal podium from the floor and leaned it against the wall. "Nothing going on. Where was I?"

"Talking about economics," a student near the back blurted out.

"Really? Cause I thought we were in English lit, dimwit," Geoff returned, making the class chuckle.

I turned back to my childhood best friend. I was going crazy, and it probably was because I couldn't escape Geoff. My heart throbbed, and I lost my breath again. My stomach swirled and my world seemed to be crumbling for no good reason other than I felt alone. It seemed like all eyes in the auditorium were on me, even though they weren't. I needed space. I needed to get out of there.

I folded my notebook and slipped it into my bag, tucking the desk back beside my chair. I began to slip out of the room, but Liam's warm hand gripped my wrist.

"Where are you going?"

I shrugged. "Bathroom? See you tonight."

I couldn't even force a smile as I pulled away from Liam and flew up the auditorium's steps, not looking back. I took the steps two by two, and dashed out the lecture hall door, taking a sharp right around the corner.

My forehead slammed into someone's chin.

He stepped away, rubbing his square jaw.

"I'm so sorry! Are you okay?" My eyes assessed for damages. No blood. No redness to his heavily tanned skin.

He dropped his hand. "I'm fine."

"Were you going in?" I stepped out of his way.

He shook his head, causing his matted blond hair to slip from behind his ear. "I'm not in that class." My heart was still fluttering from the panic I had just experienced, or from the piercing green eyed stare from the man in front of me. He was a few years older than me, but he wasn't like any of the other college students. His hair was dirty and so were his clothes. Beige and loose-fitting fabric that looked as if he was in a medieval period play or heading to a Renaissance fair.

I swallowed a lump. Had Luke been afraid of him?

And if Luke was afraid, maybe I should be, too.

I shook that thought away. Luke wasn't real.

There's no way he could be.

The man smiled with a charming gleam in his eye, like he wanted to know more about me, but now wasn't the time.

"I should have learned by now to watch where I'm going." I waved and took off down the hallway, heading towards the nearest exit.

Under the bright fall sun with distance between me and the business school building, I felt a bit better. No man wearing an old-fashioned costume and no dragon in sight. Luke had to be a figment of my imagination due to the stressors in my life right now: losing my mom, selling my childhood home, breaking up with my long-term boyfriend, moving away, and starting college to name a few. I didn't have anyone I could talk to about any of those situations, so I brought back my old best friend.

What other explanation was there?

I tended to keep things inside and hide my feelings, and I had to open up to someone. My sanity depended on it.

My one good girlfriend—Sonja—lived two hours away, back in Arcola. We had a tradition, whenever I was so angry at Geoff for doing something stupid and I couldn't take it anymore, she'd take me down to the Steak & Shake and buy me the biggest, most expensive ice cream malt they had while I told her all my troubles. Well, maybe I could do it over the phone. It wouldn't be the same, but if there was a shot that it would make Luke go away, it'd be worth it.

I'd call her tonight, before heading to Young Monsters with Liam and Kat. Besides, Sonja started her freshman year of college yesterday, too, and I should see how her day had gone. Hopefully, not quite as exciting as mine.

Chapter 6

I made it through the remaining three classes I had and headed to my dorm to call Sonja and get ready for a night on the town. I had been in Bloomington for nearly a month already and hadn't seen anything except a coffee shop, a little convenience store, and a few other buildings on campus. Getting out was a good thing. College was a time of new experiences, and Young Monsters' dance club was definitely something different.

It'd be great, as long as I didn't see my own little monster with beady red eyes, golden scales, and four-inch horns. Seeing imaginary creatures was not normal. I had that realization many years ago, and after admitting it, Luke had finally gone away.

While organizing my backpack for tomorrow, I called Sonja.

"Hey girl, I miss you!" she exclaimed, answering the phone.

"I missed you too! How's life?" No sense in diving into all my problems first. She had always been my sounding board, and I didn't want to take advantage of that. Maybe that's why I hadn't called her right after Geoff broke up with me. Or, perhaps I was in denial.

"Oh, same old, same old. You know, going to school, parents still enforcing a curfew of ten PM even though I'm in college. You don't know how lucky you are."

Lucky? Humpf.

Sonja's voice was apologetic. "I didn't mean that like how it sounded. I know you don't have anyone to enforce a curfew. I just meant that you went away to college. Oh, Ruby. I'm so sorry."

I laughed. "Don't worry. I know you didn't mean anything by it." It wasn't my situation with family life that bothered me right now.

"It's just that I thought that starting college meant I was an adult, but living at home, I realize that'll never happen. Mom asks when I'll be home for dinner, while Dad makes sure I'm not one minute late."

"But you're eighteen. Almost nineteen."

"I know, but Dad says his sleep is disrupted if I'm not home, so I get a curfew as long as I live with them. These will be the longest two years of my life!" Sonja chose to go to the local community college for the first two years because she didn't know where else she'd like to go. It bought her time to make that decision and not throw money away.

"Everything good with Ollie?" I asked. Sonja had been dating Ollie since prom. They had gone to the same high school for four years and never talked, then one day, the magic happened—so to speak. I had nothing to do with it.

"Yeah, he's good." Ollie chose to not go off to college. He had said that the country was short on skilled trade workers, so he took a position as a plumber's apprentice right after school ended. Maybe that was part of why Sonja stayed so close to home. "How about Geoff?"

I cringed. Here we go. I wasn't ready to face it, but, as Geoff had said, I just had to rip the Band-Aid off. "How much time do you have?"

She laughed. "All night." Just like old times, only we were on the phone instead of dipping mini-fries into ice cream.

My chest constricted and I fought a quiver in my voice

as I admitted the words out loud. "We broke up." Okay, that was a truth stretch. "Actually, he dumped me." There it was. The cold, hard truth, and hopefully, my imaginary dragon would go away.

"Oh, Ruby. When? I'm so sorry."

"It happened two days ago. I've been a bit mopey since then and didn't want to talk about it—especially since Geoff seems to have a new girlfriend already."

"What? How is that possible? That scumbag."

"Yup, I know. I've been so angry that I can't focus." Maybe angry wasn't the right word. I felt...used. Not-appreciated. I felt like I was a burden he had for all this time. That I had made him miserable.

Sonja was silent a bit, then her voice softened. "It's not what you want to hear, but it's something my dad always says. Sometimes, forgiveness is the best medicine. Don't occupy yourself with Geoff. *He's* not your problem. You can only take care of yourself. You need to forgive, forget, and move on."

"I am. I'm actually going out tonight. It should make me feel a little better."

"Did you make friends already? Of course, you did. People gravitate your way. It's like magic."

"Magic, huh?" I laughed, but then stopped when an image of the blotches on Geoff's cheek filled my head. How long do I let his skin look like that before I try to fix it? Right now, I wasn't feeling too forgiving. "Tell me all the details of your new routine. How are your professors? Classes?" Okay, I changed the subject. I may have admitted what happened to Sonja, but I didn't want to dig deep down in my emotions for fear I'd start crying again.

Sonja and I chatted for over an hour, comparing our

schools and reminiscing about high school life. Finally, I realized I needed to be at Young Monsters in an hour and ended the call, but not before promising that we'd chat more often. It was going to be our Wednesday night routine.

When we hung up, I felt better. I really did. The sense of dread in the pit of my stomach was dissipating, and I realized, my life wasn't over. Geoff was only a small portion of who I was. In fact, Geoff didn't make me who I was at all.

* * *

I was a bit late to Young Monsters—very unlike me. Kat and Liam were sitting at a bar, having a soda. Twenty or thirty people moved their bodies to the beat on a pulsing dance-floor as music blared through the speakers. I guess no one came here to socialize.

I pushed my way up to the bar and my two new friends turned around and smiled. Liam stood, wrapping his arms around me in a friendly hug. His lips grazed my ear as he shouted to overcome the music. "You made it! I'm happy to see you." He motioned for me to take his seat. When he slipped a menu down in front of me and said something, I didn't hear him.

I tried to tell him that, but couldn't get my voice loud enough, so I just smiled. He jetted his head towards the dance floor, mouthing, "Wanna dance?" but I had just gotten there and needed a minute. I wasn't a dancer, but I'd try.

I held up the menu and said, "After a drink."

Kat stood up and took his hand, dragging him through the crowd to an empty spot where she jerked her body in an odd dance. I laughed, pleased that she wasn't shy, but a tinge jealous at the same time.

When the bartender came over, I pointed to an orange juice and grenadine concoction and soon, was sipping something delicious. When I turned back to the dance floor, a little, shiny dragon was weaving between everyone's feet.

I rubbed my eyes.

Luke was still there. So much for working through my stress with Sonja. Maybe there was something more in the drink besides grenadine. I stiffened in my seat as Luke danced. The little dragon lifted on his hind legs, balancing with his tail, and pumped his arms with the music. His wide hips swayed, and soon, his tail thumped against the ground. When he looked at me and gave me a toothy smile, I burst out laughing. I lifted my drink to my lips. Maybe having an imaginary friend wasn't so bad.

Luke continued to dance, circling everyone's feet, and at the point where he turned around and shook his tail at me, I struggled not to spit out my orange juice. Luke wiggled his way through the crowd, and eventually I couldn't see him anymore. I turned back to the bar and set my drink on the polished wood. I took a deep breath, trying to overcome the social anxiety I had. No excuses. It was time to dance. If Luke could do it…and the terrible-dancer, Kat, so could I.

I slid from my chair with the last bit of drink in my hand. With the straw in my mouth, I began to suck the rest down as I spun around, but I slammed into a broad chest, spilling the juice concoction down both our shirts.

His dirty blond hair brushed his cheek, and his curvy-lipped frown quickly righted itself as our eyes met. He leaned in, his warm breath caressing my ear as he spoke to overcome the music. "You're making a habit of running into me."

I pulled away. "I'm so sorry!" I spun around and picked up a napkin, wiping the orange juice from his already dirty, beige—tunic? There was no other way to describe his shirt, but the huge stain stuck out on the light fabric. He pulled off a messenger bag that crossed his chest and wiped the thick leather strap. Oh, I wished this wouldn't have happened.

He leaned forward again. "You said you were sorry last time you bumped into me, but I don't mind."

I shook my head. If only I had left my juice on the bar. I picked up more napkins and blotted his shirt again. The red grenadine would stain. After failing to soak up the stain, I realized the man just stood there—no doubt enjoying my hands on his chest.

Dumb, innocent, Ruby.

I dropped my hands.

Maybe I shouldn't have come here tonight. At least, I should have been more careful. I looked at my blue t-shirt, noticing the big purplish stain down the front. Once more, I wished I never spilled the OJ.

My pocket grew warm, and I remembered the medallion.

Oh, no.

Not more magic.

It had never been so responsive.

What was going on?

I looked down at the stain on the guy's chest, and it disappeared right in front of me. The stain on my shirt disappeared too.

He looked at me with his jaw wide open and his green eyes flashed with surprise.

Instantly, my eyelids grew heavy, and I held back a

yawn. This stranger had seen me do magic and there was no taking it back.

"I'm sorry, I gotta go!" I turned away from him. Turned away from Kat and from Liam, and headed out the door, needing to crawl into my bed and hide from the world. I needed to figure out how to control my magic.

First, I hexed Geoff.

Then did magic in front of a complete stranger.

What consequences would there be if this world found out magic was real?

My mom had passed along my father's warning, and, for once, I trusted his words.

I had to get control of the magic that ran through my veins.

Chapter 7

Still exhausted, I awoke the next morning to dragon breath—literally! Luke stood on my chest with his toothy grin and wagging tail in a way that reminded me of my childhood when he wanted to play. When I was little, he seemed so much bigger. It appeared Luke hadn't grown at all in the past decade, even though I did.

I moaned and pushed him off me. "I'm all grown up now." I didn't play with an imaginary friend.

Luke hopped down on the floor and picked up a dirty sock, flipping it at me with his mouth. The sock hit me in the shoulder. Perhaps I wasn't losing my mind. I was a witch— even if only one-quarter witch. Magic was real and perhaps dragons were real, too. I found the sock on my bed and tossed it back at Luke. His little wings beat, and he caught it midair.

If Luke was imaginary, how did he toss me the sock? I dragged my hands down my face. Was I imagining everything? "Are you real?" I asked him. I felt like an idiot, but Luke shook his head yes. I patted his cool scales between his horns. "Of course, you think you're real." The question was, did I? And what did it all mean?

"Why, out of billions of people on this planet, are you here with me?"

He looked up and blinked his big, innocent eyes at me. "Because I'm the only witch in this world, right? The only one who can see you?"

Luke seemed to shrug.

I forced myself out of bed, not wanting to face the day after abandoning everyone at Young Monsters last night, but I couldn't hide forever. Luke tossed the sock at me again, but I dodged it. "I have to get to school. This will have to wait."

My dragon shot me sad, puppy dog eyes, but I ignored them and gathered my clothes and supplies for a shower.

After getting ready for the day, I returned to my room and Luke was gone. This was typical behavior of him. There one moment, gone the next. When I was a child, his disappearances used to disappoint me. Now, I found myself relieved. I didn't need the distraction or the trouble Luke brought, and even if he was real, it's not like he could teach me how to control my magic.

* * *

I arrived to economics class fifteen minutes early, and as I descended the steps, I debated finding a different seat and avoiding Kat and Liam since I bailed on them last night. I didn't though. At some point I'd need to face the music, so why not get it out of the way? Not that I would have the opportunity to avoid them. Liam was right behind me as I scooted down the aisle to my seat.

"Where did you go last night?" he asked.

"I spilled my drink down my shirt." Nothing like admitting your failures. "I snuck out before anyone noticed." None of that was a lie, I just left out the part where I used a bit of magic to fix my clumsiness.

Liam didn't seem happy with that answer, and I didn't blame him.

"I should have let you know I was leaving, but…I didn't." I could have inserted some small white lie here, but why?

After Liam and I were situated in our seat, he looked at

me as if he could see through the truth I was withholding. "How about we try again? This time, just you and me. Someplace a bit quieter so we can chat?"

That was it. It was a clear invitation for a date even after disappearing on him last night. I nodded—way too eagerly, and I toned it down some. "That sounds like fun."

"Good. What's your number?" He pulled out his phone and swiped the screen a few times.

It was a date. A real, real date. I rattled off my phone number and as soon as Liam typed it in his phone, mine received a text:

Unknown: *Hi* :-)

"That's me," he whispered. "I'll call or text you more info later. How about tomorrow night? Unless you already have plans for a Friday evening?"

"No plans. It sounds good." I could use something to distract me from this week. If every week at college was like this, there was no way I'd survive—and this one was only four days long.

Kat slipped in her seat behind me. She didn't say anything about my disappearance last night. Maybe she was happy to have the time with the handsome Liam. If the shoes were reversed, I know I would have been pleased.

The lecture started, and I hadn't even glanced Geoff's way this morning. I smiled at my strength, but the longer I focused on the professor, the less I could concentrate. Was he holding hands with the redhead? Whispering in her ear? I needed just one quick peek.

Geoff's cheek had a huge white bandage on it, covering

where the small bumps were yesterday.

My heart thumped.

What had I done?

Maybe he was just embarrassed of his imperfections. It couldn't be that bad, right? I looked again, but didn't see anything around the bandage.

The professor's words could have been in a foreign language for the rest of class because I didn't hear a word he said. I went through all sorts of panic situations. What if Geoff's wound spread? Ate away his face? What if I could never get control of my magic and did something far, far worse to someone else?

By the end of class, I was certain I'd fail out of school. Not only couldn't I pay attention, but I missed all the notes all week. I'd have to hit the textbook hard—or maybe Liam or Kat would let me read their notes. Did I need to skip my date with Liam tomorrow to study?

Again, I couldn't focus. I stared at my blank paper, knowing I needed to figure out a way to stay attentive if I was going to survive college life. Between my mind on my foolishness for dating Geoff so long, trying to figure out where I stood with Liam, my magic powers with a mind of their own, and Luke coming back, there seemed like no hope to squeeze in actual school work. At least, for the first time in months, my grief about my mom or concerns about owning a home weren't consuming me.

* * *

More than twenty-four hours passed without me seeing Luke, and I was grateful he wasn't distracting me or making me wonder if I was hallucinating. All evening was devoted to studying, and I could focus on a routine that would make me successful. I had a date with Liam, and Geoff was the last thing on my mind. I was figuring things out and my life was starting to resemble something normal.

Walking into economics, I felt that my destiny was in my hands…until I glanced to Geoff's empty seat beside the redhead.

The professor straightened his grey sports coat that matched his hair and leaned into the microphone, beginning his lecture on bear and bull markets. I couldn't focus on the front of the room. I scanned the lecture hall, but couldn't find Geoff.

Had his face gotten worse?

As soon as class ended, I jumped up, ignoring Kat's question about my weekend plans. I flew across the room, catching the redhead before she got out of her desk.

"Hi." My word was shyer than I wanted, but I was filled with insecurities. Did she know who I was? Had Geoff told her of how he felt sorry for me and dated me out of charity?

She arched an eyebrow, seemingly oblivious.

I pointed to the seat next to her. "I was wondering where Geoff was today."

Her mahogany colored lips turned down into a frown. "He texted this morning. Said he needed to go to the doctor for the sore on his cheek."

My body stiffened, but I nodded and turned away. I took the steps two by two, needing to escape. Needing somewhere to hide.

Geoff was at the doctor because of me.

I had hexed Geoff—seriously hexed him.

How far would the magic go?

Would it eat his face off?

Sweat formed on my palms as images of a giant hole in Geoff's cheek filled my mind. Would it ever heal, or would he always be scarred? I had been bitter. Childish. And I didn't like it. Sure, I had blamed it on my out-of-control magic, but it was *me* who wished Geoff the skin problem.

Maybe that's why Luke was back. Taunting me about my immaturity. Inside, I laughed a humorless laugh and shook my head at myself.

Sure, I hated Geoff for what he had done, but we still had a few good years together. He had given me the support I needed through my mom's ordeal, and no matter what, I was grateful.

I needed to fix what I did.

"Ruby, wait!"

I spun around to Liam.

"You didn't respond to my text. Does five PM work?"

I pulled out my phone and read the text:

Liam: *Five PM. Dinner at Prego's and a walk along the river.*

Did that give me enough time to finish my classes, get ready, and un-hex my ex? I surely hoped so. "Yup, that's great. Where do I meet you?"

"What dorm are you in? I'll pick you up at the entrance."

I nodded. "Einstein Hall."

He laughed. "Of course, that'd be yours."

Yup, I chose the nerdy one. Nothing wrong with that.

* * *

My classes passed by in a blur, and by four, I was back in my dorm. Luke eagerly bounced on my bed—like old times.

"Not tonight, unless you can tell me how to fix Geoff?" Luke didn't stop bouncing, and I dismissed him with a wave of my hand, pulling the medallion from my pocket. I rubbed the dragon head between my fingers.

How was I going to fix Geoff? I rubbed the coin, thinking about Geoff's once perfect skin, wishing away the magic that caused the lesions on his face. I hoped he was healed, imagined his clear complexion, and the coin heated until I could no longer hold it in my hand. It dropped on my bed.

When I yawned, I knew that was all I could do. I picked up the coin, but before I slipped it into my pocket, I hesitated.

Mom had made me promise to always keep it with me, but now, it seemed to be causing more trouble than good. I did who-knew-what to Geoff's face, and I did an act of magic in front of a complete stranger. What was next?

I opened my small jewelry box on my desk and plopped the coin inside. I was going out with Liam tonight and didn't need anything to go wrong. I wanted a normal life. College was a time of fresh starts, and I was determined to have mine after everything I had been through in the past year.

I brushed my hair and refastened it back in a ponytail. I smiled and tried to look flirty, but looked more like an over-eager child. Had I read into things with Liam and this wasn't actually a date? Toning down my excitement and looking the same as when I went to school was in my best interest. If this wasn't a date, I didn't want Liam thinking that I thought this was more than it was. Oh, I was confusing myself now.

My hand hesitated on the mascara I pulled out. I hardly ever wore makeup, but I painted my eyelashes anyway. Even if it wasn't a date, what harm did a little mascara do?

When I looked presentable, I patted Luke on the head, and, with butterflies in my stomach, I headed downstairs to wait for Liam.

Chapter 8

Any reservations I had that my evening with Liam was not a date vanished as soon as he walked up to my dorm's entrance, holding a colorful mix of flowers.

"I brought you these." He held the bouquet out to me in the center of the dorm's lobby with a smooth smile. The few other students sitting at the furniture in the area stared, and I didn't know if I should be proud, or hide.

In the entire three years Geoff and I had dated, I never received flowers. I didn't know what to do with them. Did I carry them around all evening? While contemplating my next move, I smelled their fragrant aroma, overpowered by the rose in the center. "They're beautiful, thank you."

"I'll wait here if you want to run them to your room."

I nodded. Problem solved.

When I returned downstairs from my dorm—which had no trace of Luke anymore—Liam stood right outside the giant glass entry doors, leaning against the brick building and watching the cars pass.

"I'm all set." I took a spot next to him, enjoying the perfect evening. The sun was dipping below the buildings, casting long shadow on the sidewalks and keeping the temperature just perfect for my t-shirt and jeans.

"Great. Prego's is five blocks away or so. You okay with the walk?"

I held up a foot and wiggled it. "I wore my Converse just for the occasion."

He laughed and led me to the stoplight on the corner. "What are your plans for the weekend?"

"Studying economics…actually, studying for all my classes. I haven't brought my best game to college this week. I want to work ahead some."

He coughed. "Nerd."

"Hey. I'm paying for this education. I might as well get the most out of it." I tried to look serious, but held back a smile. To me, being a nerd was a compliment. Both Sonja and I had girl crushes on Hermione Granger.

"Your parents' aren't helping you out?" When I cringed, Liam's eyes widened, and he looked away. "Sorry. It must be a touchy subject."

Here it came. My trying-to-live-a-normal-life bubble popped. "My mom died earlier this year, and my dad…well, he might as well be dead. I never met him."

I expected a long string of I'm sorrys to come, but instead, I got, "My folks aren't around either."

We were silent for the rest of the five blocks. Had I ruined our date by bringing up my parents? I should have just said they were paying for school. I mean, the trust fund my mom had *was* paying all my school-related expenses for the next few years, so it wasn't a lie.

"Here we are." Liam nodded up to a green and white striped overhang with red letters that read Prego's. "Hope you like Italian."

"Who doesn't? I could literally eat pasta until I exploded." Well, that wasn't quite true, but once, Sonja and I had tried at an all-you-can-eat pasta buffet. All we got out of it was being too tired to drive home, pulling our car over at a rest stop and taking a nap. Mom had been so mad that I missed curfew. Sonja's dad? He probably still hadn't forgiven her.

Once Liam and I were seated and had our meal ordered,

the ice clanked in my glass as I took a drink. The silence had me shifting in my seat and focusing on my cup instead of the guy in front of me. Maybe I needed to start the conversation.

"So…Liam. Tell me about yourself. I don't know anything, really, except you're taking economics, your parents aren't in the picture, and you're pretty fun to kiss." I winked, thinking I was brave for throwing that out there, but then my cheeks heated like my medallion had earlier.

He smiled. Mission accomplished: ice broken. "I'm not that exciting. I'm almost twenty-one, go to school here even though I'm not sure what I want to be when I grow up, and I like to dance, but you knew that already. Oh, and I love collecting things." His eyes lit up like there was a secret he wasn't telling me.

"Like what?"

He shrugged. "A few different things. Old books, watches," he held up his wrist to show me an old-fashioned type watch with gears on the face and a brown leather band, "and I have a pretty big collection of stones."

"Wow. I wish I had that kind of passion. Maybe you can show me some of your collections sometime."

"Are you asking to come back to my place?" His eyes widened in an expectant way and he laughed. "You're quite forward, aren't you?"

"No—that's not what I meant. I'm sorry."

"No need." He dismissed me with his hand. "I'm enjoying you. You're a bit…quirky—which is a good thing! So, tell me about yourself. All I know is that you don't pay attention in economics, have one hell of a nerdy t-shirt collection, you don't have any parents, either, and you're pretty fun to kiss, too."

I smiled that great big childish smile I had seen in the mirror earlier. "If I'm forward, then I'd call you smooth. Real smooth."

"So, what makes you who you are?"

I shrugged. What was there to tell about me? "I'm pretty boring. Spent lots of time with my ex, doing things he liked—mostly all things related to football. I just liked being with him, so I didn't mind. Oh, I'm breaking a first date rule. No talking about exes."

"You can talk about whatever you like."

"Well, I don't like talking about him, but I haven't really discovered who I am yet." Other than a witch, but I couldn't tell him that.

"That's what college is for."

I nodded. "It's not like I'm empty. I've just been busy taking care of my mom and the house she left me, that I haven't had time for much else."

"I know what you mean. Being an adult sucks, doesn't it?"

I laughed. "Yeah, maybe it does. Why did I want to grow up so bad?" Even when I was five, and pushed Luke away, all I wanted to do was be an adult. Luke used to bounce on my piano keys, making me mess up my simple songs when I first started lessons. I'd get so mad and tell him to be serious. My eyes lifted to Liam. "Oh, I do have a hobby. I play the piano. At least, I played the piano. I haven't in…well…" since Mom died, but I wasn't going there.

He raised an eyebrow.

"I took lessons since I was five. I'm pretty good," I bragged.

The waitress set a giant plate of chicken alfredo in front

of me and lasagna for Liam. We spent the rest of dinner chatting about nothing and everything, and I couldn't help but think how nice this was. It was normal.

Liam paid the bill and took my hand to lead me outside. "Now, for the second part of our date. A walk along the river."

"I didn't know there was a river here."

"It's small. More like a creek, but there's a little worn path from foot traffic."

Liam led me a few blocks away, then down a grassy bank to a small dirt trail that ran along the bank of a stream. We wound through a park, crossing under a bridge on a narrow concrete path, and the moon reflected in the rippling water.

"It's beautiful," I said.

Liam shook his head, taking my hand and pulling me close. He brushed a few loose strands of hair off my face. "No, you are."

It was a cheesy line, but it still brought butterflies to my stomach. I looked away, but he tilted my chin up, planting a kiss on my lips.

His style was the same as last time, calculated and planned, but unlike the coffee shop, he hung on much longer. When I started to compare his kiss to Geoff's, noting the different angle of my head and the different arm position, I pulled away. Images of the bandage on Geoff's cheek filled my head, and I stiffened. I had hexed him. He could be in the hospital and here I was, out enjoying myself.

I pushed Liam back a step. "I need to get home and study."

"Sorry, was I the one being too forward now?"

"No, not at all. It's just our first date." My mouth snapped shut. "It is a date, right?"

Liam nodded. "Of course it is, and it isn't really our first date. We had the coffee shop, and the dance club. Do you really have that much school work? We've only had classes for a week."

"I do. Remember, nerd here." I pointed my thumbs at my chest, then climbed back up the bank to the sidewalk on the street above us. "This was really nice."

Liam seemed to accept my excuse. It's not like I could tell him Geoff was on my mind, even if my thoughts were on the wound I inflicted upon him. "I'm glad you had a good time."

"I did." It was probably the first real, adult date I had ever had. With Geoff, it'd been watching TV, school dances, football games, and hanging out at the mall. Today with Liam was something different. I got flowers, we went out to a nice dinner where he paid, and a moonlit walk.

We may have said growing up sucked, but that wasn't true. There were good parts about it, too. Like dating.

But was I ready?

I couldn't even kiss him without thinking about another man.

Chapter 9

Today was day number two of my attempt to live a normal life, and things were looking good. I awoke late this Saturday, and Luke was nowhere to be seen. After feeling so lonely after my mom passed, it was nice having my dragon friend around, imaginary or not, but I wanted a normal life and Luke didn't fit into that plan.

I showered, then gathered up my dirty clothes from a pile on the bottom of my closet. I had over a week's worth of laundry. Since moving to Bloomington, Geoff and I had been washing our clothes together, but now, I was on my own.

I packed my computer in my backpack along with my economics notes—what little I had. There was a laundromat two blocks from here and waiting for the machines to do their job gave me a perfect time for studying. I squished everything into my laundry bag, flung it over my shoulder, and before I knew it, I was outside in the sunlight, waiting on the corner of my block for the light to flash walk.

A familiar tanned face stared at me from across the street. This was the third time I ran into him, even though we had no classes together and I didn't even know his name. The walk signal illuminated, and I debated heading the opposite way, but he had spotted me already. I took a deep breath and headed into the crosswalk.

As I passed the stranger with the greenest eyes I had ever seen, I smiled and pulled the first words I could from my head to break the ice. "I promise I won't bump into you this time."

He spun around mid-intersection, causing his long hair

to fall out from behind an ear, and walked beside me. "You sure?" He chuckled as he pushed his clumpy bangs off his face, following me to the curb he had just been standing on. "I don't know if I could take another beating from you."

"Hey, hey, hey. You don't look too beaten up. I must have taken it easy on you." I examined his chin where we bumped into each other earlier this week. It was completely fine, but I noticed a small cleft he had at the bottom of his chin that was a bit charming. But then, I remembered spilling my drink on him—and making the stain just disappear. No wonder he followed me. I swallowed and kept moving towards the laundromat. "It's nice seeing you, but I gotta do some laundry." I patted my bag, smiled, and focused on moving forward.

He didn't get the hint, jogging up next to me. Was he wearing the same costume of a tunic and beige pants from earlier this week? "Can we talk?" His face was stone serious.

I shook my head. "I have studying to do."

"It won't take long."

I stopped. My heart raced. What would I say to his questions about how the drink spill had vanished?

"Not here," he said. "Somewhere more…private?"

I swallowed. He had noticed the stain's disappearance. How could he not? If I was him, I'd want an explanation. I'd want confirmation of what I saw—to make sure I wasn't crazy. My day number two of being normal quickly faded away. "Let me get my clothes started. The laundromat's just up ahead." Honestly, I was stalling. I needed time to think of a logical explanation to what he saw.

We disappeared into the brick building and the scent of floral soap stung my nose. I found an empty machine and stuffed my clothes inside, but realized Blond Boy was right behind me, watching me pull out my underwear. I lifted the bag and carefully dumped everything discreetly into the big drum and shut the cover. I stopped, feeling my chest tighten. I wasn't prepared for life. I didn't bring any soap, and I didn't bring my spare change. Geoff had always taken care of that.

A student leaned on the machine next to mine with a giant tub of detergent. "Can I borrow some soap?"

She nodded and pushed the container my way. Next issue, change.

"What's your name, anyway?" I asked Blond Boy.

He pushed himself close to me, lazily leaning on the washing machine I had just dumped all my dirty underwear in. "Ty."

"Well, Ty, do you have any change?" The request wasn't out of line. He was the one who wanted to talk to me. If he had just kept walking, he'd be $1.25 richer.

He pulled out a handful of coins from his pocket and slowly picked through it, but before he handed over some quarters, he pulled them back. "I'll give these to you in exchange for your name."

I held out my hand. "Ruby."

He smiled and dropped five quarters into my palm.

Once the machine was humming with running water and my head full of all sorts of excuses for my little act of magic, I crossed my arms over my chest ready for his questions. "Okay, I'm all yours."

He arched an eyebrow, turning my simple words into an innuendo. One that made my heart skip a beat in a way that was new. Oh my, my hormones were out of control. I reminded myself I had a perfect date with Liam only last night, but Ty was cute, there was no denying that, in an I-might-end-up-in-prison-but-you'll-have-fun-the-whole-time kind of way.

He eyed the empty study cubicles along the outer edge of the room, and I followed him into one, slipping ourselves all the way inside.

"How did you get here?" Ty asked, pulling his messenger bag off and setting it down beside him.

Now it was my turn to arch an eyebrow. That was not the question I expected. "What do you mean?"

"Here. In this realm. Living amongst the non-magical."

A lump grew in my throat. Did Ty know about magic? What did that mean? I wasn't ready to trust him and let him into my world. I spent months keeping my secret. "I don't know what you mean."

"I don't believe you. Why are you following me?"

"Following you?" I laughed. "You're the one who's following me." The lump in my throat grew bigger. Maybe it wasn't a coincidence that I spilled my drink on him. He knew I was a witch. I tightened my lips, not willing to offer him anything. He was the one who came for information.

He tilted his chin and leaned on the table, uncomfortably close. "I am not following *you*." He emphasized the word you in a way that made me wonder who he was following. "I didn't know you were magical until Young Monsters, but there's no denying it."

I tensed my jaw, curious, but not willing to admit anything. "Is that why you approached me at Young Monsters? You thought I was…magical?"

The corner of his lip curved up into a grin, revealing a solitary dimple. "No. I came up to you because you were smiling and laughing, and I recognized you. I wanted to say hi.

It wasn't until you cleaned up your spilled drink that I realized you were something else."

Was he a threat? Mom said I wasn't supposed to tell anyone about my abilities. She also said to keep the medallion close, but look where that got me.

I still chose to avoid the truth. "I grew up in Illinois. I've only been here a few weeks."

He shook his head. "You really don't know what I'm talking about, do you?" He ran his fingers through his hair and leaned back into the booth, blowing out a breath. "Ahh, never mind."

He scooted out of the bench seat and grabbed his bag. "For what it's worth, you have a beautiful smile."

With that, he started to walk away.

"Wait!" I called, but stopped myself. If he left, would I ever see him again? Could he give me some answers about magic and witches and…perhaps…dragons?

He stopped and spun around, revealing a grin that said he was getting his way. I couldn't help but admire his striking smile, with a row of straight, white teeth. I debated telling him the truth about everything, but I bit my tongue. Instead, I settled with, "Do you have any more quarters? I still need to dry my clothes." I was a coward. There was no other explanation.

He tilted his chin, and I held out my hand, holding my ground.

He dropped his head, shaking it, but pulled a handful of change from his pocket. As he picked a quarter up, I saw a familiar tarnished medallion.

How'd he get that?

My insides clenched with anger. Had he stolen it?

How'd he get into my room? "Where'd you get this?" I swooped up the silver medallion and held it up, examining the familiar dragon emblem. My piece of silver had an electrical tingle, but now, it seemed like nothing more than a giant coin. Had he done something to my medallion? Changed it somehow?

"It's mine." His teeth grit tight.

"I—I don't believe you." My heart sped up, and I picked up my backpack, ignoring my clothes in the washer and holding the medallion tightly in my hand. Either he stole it, or had another one just like it. My medallion came from my dad, and if Ty had another one, it meant he might somehow be connected to my father.

I rushed out of the laundromat towards my dorm, hearing Ty right behind me. He couldn't know my dad, could he? He had to have stolen my medallion, there was no other explanation.

So much for my normal, no magic day.

Chapter 10

Ty's rhythmic footsteps were right behind me as I ran down the sidewalk and climbed the six flights of stairs to my dorm room, and I didn't care. All I cared about was seeing if what he said was true.

If his silver coin was a duplicate medallion, that meant Ty was somehow connected to my father. Not that I cared, since dear old Dad abandoned us, leaving Mom to care for a child with powers she knew nothing about. Still, my father was the only connection I had to the magic blood that flowed in my veins.

Breathing heavily, I flung open the cover to my jewelry box, revealing the familiar tarnished silver. My nerves settled, but curiosity consumed me as I held both medallions up to each other, admiring their similarities, but also their differences.

They weren't the same. The front had the same dragon that looked remarkably like Luke, with slanted eyes, a deep forehead ending in horns, delicate wings, and a thick tail, but the writing on the back was different. Symbols twisted around both medallions in a spiral pattern from the outside to the inside, covering the entire surface.

"Where'd you get that?" Ty called from behind me.

I spun around to see him leaning lazily against my door frame. He hadn't stepped inside my room, yet he watched my every move. "Me?" I palmed my coin, hiding it. "Where did yours come from?"

"I asked first, and you're the one who stole my coin."

I huffed, but spit out the truth. "It's from my father.

You?"

Ty reached into his pocket and pulled out a handful of change. Mixed in with dimes and pennies were a few more silver medallions. I set the two I had down on my desk and snatched three more of them from his hand. I laid the five pieces of silver out in a row, noticing Ty's four all had identical patterns of symbols on the back, mine being the only different one.

My heart dropped a little. Maybe Ty had no connection with my father at all.

"So, where did you get yours from?" I asked again.

Ty entered my room and stood over my shoulder.

"From the cave dragons."

Cave dragons?

What did he know about dragons? Maybe I wasn't crazy at all...or both of us were.

Ty rubbed his fingernails against his chest and blew them off. "Yup. Stole the treasure myself."

Treasure?

My brain couldn't keep up. Was this a joke? If it was, someone would have had to know about my medallion. Would have had to know about my friend, Luke.

I picked up my piece of silver and sat down in my desk chair, rubbing my finger across the tarnished surface. How was this possible? Did I believe Ty?

If I hadn't known my father was a witch, I would have dismissed this as a coincidence and not believed a word Ty said, but I knew better. I examined Ty, trying to get a feel for his character—not that looks meant anything, but he didn't look dishonest. What did dishonesty even look like? His blond hair was a mess, like he didn't spend much time combing it and it hadn't been washed in days, but he tucked it behind his ear to keep it out of his eyes. He wasn't much taller than me, but his shoulders were wide, and his torso muscular—in an athletic way. Like someone that participated in one of those ninja warrior competitions. He was older than me, but not that much. Maybe twenty-one? Twenty-two at the most, and he was wearing the same clothes I had seen him in a few days ago.

And he knew of dragons. And treasures.

And, I was certain, witches, too.

I swallowed the lump in my throat. Turning my medallion in my hand, my eyes fixated on the dragon. If Ty knew of all these things, maybe he knew a little about magic. Maybe he was a witch, himself? Could he at least make sure I never inadvertently hexed anyone else again but still let me learn how to use my powers? Control them?

Could I tell him—a complete stranger—my secret?

I took a deep breath.

I had dated Geoff for three years and thought I loved him, but kept my secret from him. Mom made me promise…

But she wasn't here anymore, was she? And neither was my dad. He was never here to begin with. Why have powers if they were not meant to be used?

Ty pushed his hair off his face, tucking his bangs behind his ears and looking at me with focused green eyes. He blew out a breath. "I need help. I need to get back home but can't find the portal."

The portal?

Sweat threatened my skin. I was ignorant of the world Ty described, and it appeared he thought I knew more than I did. Was he dangerous to me? I laughed at myself. The biggest threat in the room was me—I was the one who sent Geoff to the hospital.

I slipped my medallion back into my pocket and handed Ty his coins. "I'm sorry, but I don't know what you're talking about. I wish I could help."

His shoulders slouched, and he leaned back against my bed, tilting his chin and arching an eyebrow at me, like he was assessing if I was a threat like I had done to him. "You're a witch."

So, he did know about witches. I bit my bottom lip, not denying or agreeing with what he said.

He continued. "I saw it with my own eyes. You made the stain disappear, and you cleaned my entire shirt." He motioned to the tunic he wore, which appeared brand new. He tightened his lips and assessed me from head to toe, and I fought to not wheel my chair away from him to hide my secrets that he pulled from deep inside me. "Witches are from my world, not this one. You came through the portal, too."

I coughed. "You got the wrong girl." But how much about that other side of me—the one that held my magic—could Ty teach me? He was the best opportunity I've ever had. I rolled my desk chair back, but leaned forward on my arms. Sometimes, you had to take a leap of faith. I looked away and spilled my secrets. "I was born here. My father was half witch. I don't know anything about him, since I never met him. I was raised by my mother, who was very much human."

"Was?" He caught that. "I'm sorry."

I shrugged. Everyone was sorry.

"I don't think I can help you with your portal, but maybe you could help me learn more about being a witch and about magic." My last words croaked and I fought back tears. I hadn't known how desperate I was to know who I was. Even though I despised my father for abandoning us, I still wanted to know who he was and where he came from.

I wanted to know who I was.

College was the time for finding yourself, right?

And most of all, one small little act of magic sent Geoff to the doctor.

What would I do next, if I didn't get control?

I hated to admit it, but I needed Ty.

Chapter 11

Ty scooted back on my bed, leaning against the wall with his arms behind his head, showing off his biceps. I spun my desk chair towards him, trying to keep my eyes focused on his face and not his body. "A few days ago, I was searching for a gem dragon's treasure. As I hunted one dragon, he led me into this world."

I sucked in my bottom lip, forcing myself not to say anything. Ty had been hunting a dragon…was that dragon, Luke? Could he see my imaginary friend? If so, that meant one of two things. Either Ty chased Luke right back on my doorstep or my dragon accidentally led this dragon hunter right to me. Or maybe, both things were true.

And if that was the case, did that mean Luke was real and Ty was hunting him…going to kill him? My stomach turned. If I pointed Ty in Luke's direction, it might get rid of Luke once and for all…but I also…loved him, deep down.

Ty's words pulled me out of my head. "While I was hunting the dragon, we must have passed through a magical portal into this city. My aunt used to tell me stories of a world full of people without magic. Where machines took over, and I had always thought her stories were fairy tales." He laughed. "Obviously, they were true. I followed the dragon I hunted to this enormous school…and that's when I first bumped into you. Then again at Young Monsters."

"So, you say you were hunting this dragon. Were you going to kill him?"

He laughed. "If I needed to, yes."

I clammed up. I had so many other questions, but there

was this protective nature I had regarding Luke.

Ty continued, "I know the portal home is somewhere in this city, but I'm running out of silver coins and won't survive here much longer. This place...and culture...is so unfamiliar. If I want to find this dragon, I need to do it fast or find more funding. Your world makes people pay for everything."

I swallowed, but my mouth felt like sandpaper. Was this the true reason Luke was here? Did it have nothing to do with me, but rather because Ty had chased him back into my world? I rubbed my temple. "Like I said before, I can't help you with the portal." Even though, sending Ty back home would protect Luke—and there it was. I realized that I believed my dragon was real.

Ty's eyebrows knitted together. "But you're a witch. Of course, you can open a portal."

"I'm not a real witch. I'm only one-quarter—mostly just a regular human."

"It doesn't matter how diluted your blood is. Magic is magic."

"I don't really have magic. I mean, I do, but the best I've done is repair a painting." I stood and pulled down my mom's rolled up elephant painting from on top of my bookcase. I unwrapped it, examining its perfection. The tear was still gone. "And, I may have hexed my ex-boyfriend...just a little." My heartbeat amplified with that confession, but it felt good to admit it out loud.

Ty tilted his chin and a sly smile tugged at his curvy lips. "You hexed an ex-boyfriend?"

"I mean, he deserved it. Dumped me for another girl right before school started last weekend. Now, he might be in the hospital with a wound I caused." That was what happened, wasn't it? As simple as that. "I didn't mean for something bad to happen to him, but my private thoughts got carried away. He's now in the hospital, I think."

"Only a child is that careless."

"Hey, it's like I'm a child. I just learned I was a witch five months ago."

Ty squinted at me, but let that comment go. "The trouble with magic is it needs balance and will find the stability on its own if it has to. One good deed needs one bad act to keep the equilibrium. You know the saying, nothing without consequence."

I knew that too well. I fixed mom's painting, but then gave Geoff a skin condition that put him in the hospital. My guts twisted. "So, if I removed the hex, wished it was better again…"

"It might work or it might not. Something worse could happen. The thing about the good and bad is they are specific to you. Perhaps hexing your ex was a good thing, to you, but the fact that it got out of hand was the bad. You could be even. Fixing him could also be good—that your guilt went away, or bad—that he's better. Depends on your perspective."

The sweat I had kept at bay moistened my palms and the back of my neck. I had tried to lift Geoff's hex. Was that enough of a balance or was something going to go wrong?

"Magic is a balance that all witches must carefully learn to manipulate," Ty said.

"And what about you?" I nodded towards the man on my bed, and I almost laughed at that absurdity. Who knew in less than a week, I'd go from a long-term relationship to having a strange man in my room? And that was after kissing a different man the previous day.

Ty laughed and held up his hands, palms towards me. "I don't have a drop of magic blood. Most people in my world don't. I'm just as human as pretty much everyone else in your world—well, except for you. Thank goodness. I think being a witch is more of a curse than a blessing." From what I knew, he wasn't wrong. His eyes perused my room, from the bookshelf on the far wall, to my desk, to the closet beside my bed. "Can I stay here?"

"No! Of course not!"

"I've been sleeping down at the school—the college, you called it. I've been slipping into various rooms at night and catching a few hours of rest on the hard floors. I could really use a bath and a soft bed."

"No," I repeated. "Does it look like I have any room? Plus, I only have one bed. Where would I sleep?"

He shrugged. "I'm not asking for your bed, though…" His lips turned up into that sly smile again, "I wouldn't be opposed to sharing it." He winked, and I shuddered. Not that he wasn't good looking, but his forwardness wasn't anything I was comfortable with. Had I made Liam that uncomfortable at dinner? Ty must have read my reaction, because he continued. "Come on. I was just joking. I'd be happy with a few blankets on the floor."

"No," I said for the third time. "It's against the rules." Not that I cared much for rules. Geoff had stayed here on multiple occasions since we moved in three weeks ago.

He laughed. "It's only against the rules if we get caught." He scooted to the end of the bed; his eyes wide. "I'll make you a deal."

"A deal? What do you have for me?"

He stood and found the bouquet on my desk. He stuck

his nose in, closed his eyes, and inhaled. I reminded myself that I might already have a boyfriend, and Ty staying here would ruin everything. I had kissed Liam and all, but those thoughts fluttered away when Ty held out his hand for me to shake.

"You let me stay here and help me look for the portal, and I'll help you with your magic. It's obvious you need me. I mean, you hexed your ex." He laughed, but he was right. Even now, I felt the warmth of the medallion in my pocket, wanting me to use it. Wanting me to make the next bad magic spell. And maybe Ty knew my father? Could I at least find out if he was alive or dead? I took a deep breath. Maybe he knew if my father was good or evil, since I appeared to be struggling to do the right thing. Maybe it was in my blood?

I reached out my hand and took his. It was heavily calloused, yet warm and inviting and I didn't want to let go. I sure hoped I wouldn't regret this. "Deal."

He smiled. "Great! Now point me to the nearest bath. I haven't fully cleaned myself up for two days before crossing the portal."

I looked at his filthy pants and a few smudges on his arms. It had been a hard few days for him, but he didn't smell. In fact, I'd say he even smelled...good? A bit like being outside in autumn right after the rain. His dull hair said he needed to clean up, but Einstein Hall was a female-only dorm. I don't know how I'd get him into the shower. Maybe this was more work than it was worth. "First, give me a little token of what I have in store. Teach me something so I know you can hold up your end of the bargain."

He raised an eyebrow, then folded his arms over his chest. "Okay. What do you know about magic?"

"Nothing."

He laughed. "Then this will be easy. Remember each act of magic must be balanced, or it gets out of control. Something good goes along with something bad."

I nodded for him to continue.

He tilted his chin at the flowers Liam gave me. "It's such a shame these flowers will die. Which is your favorite?"

I pointed to the little blue forget-me-nots next to the red rose. They may not be the ones with the big aroma or the prettiest in the bunch, but they were my favorite color.

"Touch it. Pull your magic and urge it to grow. To flourish. To live at the expense of the other flowers in the bouquet. Have them die and shrivel. Give their lives so the little blues ones survive."

I had no idea how to do it, but I closed my eyes, stuck my hand in my pocket and fisted the medallion, imagining nothing but the blue flowers.

"Very good." Ty said.

I opened my eyes to a wilted bouquet, except for the little blue flowers. The entire bottom of the vase was overgrown with fresh white roots.

"Now, you should plant them. They are ready to live."

"I thought you weren't magical? How'd you know that'd work?"

He laughed. "I'm not, but at home, I'm surrounded by magic." He then turned away and buried himself in my closet. "Do you have any clean clothes I can wear? Something that's not so girly?" He paged through my shirts, and I remembered my clothes I had down at the laundromat. I had to flip the clothes over to the dryer. Ty had lent me money down there, and it didn't sit right with me. He hasn't showered in days, claims he has nowhere to stay, but had a pocket full of change? And not just any change, but American money. "Where'd you get the money that I borrowed at the laundromat?"

"Silver coins seem to be as valuable in this world as mine. I took some cave dragon treasure to a place called *Guns and Pawn* and received enough money to eat, but I'm almost out. I only have those four coins you saw left."

Maybe that was believable. He seemed smart enough to figure that out. I lifted a grocery bag I had by the door, stuffed with Geoff's things I hadn't returned yet. "Dig through here. You shouldn't find anything too *girly*. Geoff's a bit bigger than you, but they should be masculine enough for your liking. And for the shower…um…this is a women only dorm."

The corner of his lip turned up in a smile. "Women only? I just found the treasure chest."

He was so different than anyone else I knew, and I found it…appealing. Urgh! What was wrong with me? "Come on. I'll stand lookout while you shower. Then we need to head down to the laundromat."

I gathered shampoo and a towel before leading him down the hall. When I peeked into the shower room, the water shut off as soon as I opened the door.

"We'll have to wait a minute or two. Someone's inside now."

Ty nodded.

"Maybe if you wash out your clothes in the shower, we can throw them in the dryer with mine." My thoughts lingered on the flower with roots back in my room. That magic had come so easy to me. Good and bad. Yin and yang. I could handle this.

Soon, a girl exited the bathroom with her hair up in a

towel. I smiled, and headed inside, leaving Ty in the hallway. The bathroom was empty, so I motioned him inside.

"What kind of bath room is this?" He asked, looking around the corner into a shower stall.

"No bath tubs here. Just showers."

He arched an eyebrow.

Had he never showered? I reached in and got the water running, then stepped outside as soon as I saw the enlightenment on his face. He closed the door and flipped his dirty clothes over the top edge, then I heard the splashing of water off his body.

Looking across the bathroom, I caught the golden skin of a familiar dragon.

"Luke?" I whispered, as I headed away from the shower and around the corner to where the sinks were located.

Luke was on top of a sink, splashing water on his face with his little arms. He looked at me, with big, red eyes, and shook his head in warning. He looked back to where Ty was showering.

What did Luke know about Ty? Maybe I shouldn't have been receptive to Ty's idea. I mean, I knew he was out hunting dragons.

"What are you saying?" I asked Luke, but already knew, he never spoke.

Leaving the water running, Luke flapped his wings and glided down to the floor. He headed towards the door and disappeared into thin air.

A knot formed in my stomach. Was I making a mistake? I took a deep breath and looked at myself in the mirror. What was the right thing to do? Why didn't I have anyone to ask that question to?

Why was I all alone?

The water shut off, and soon, the shower door squeaked open. I took a deep breath and headed back for Ty.

Stopping in my tracks, I searched for my breath that escaped me, not expecting what I saw. Ty's blond hair was much darker, clean, but plastered with water back off his face, revealing his chiseled jawline, but that wasn't the first thing I noticed. With the towel wrapped around his waist, his sculpted bare chest had me searching for air. He was all muscle, and a jagged sapphire-blue dragon tattoo ran down his pectoral, with its tail following the ropes of muscles making up his abdomen. Its wing covered his shoulder and his upper arm. The ink on his skin was tribal in nature, giving the markings a dangerous look. Water followed the same path, disappearing into the towel that hung low on his hips. Around his neck hung a necklace of some type.

I may have drooled a little.

I had been with Geoff so long that I didn't know what it was like to be attracted to someone purely for physical reasons.

That was until now.

There was something off about the dragon tattoo—and that's when I realized three wide scars cut through the center of it, almost like a giant claw had ripped at Ty's chest.

He smiled, grabbing Geoff's shirt out of the bag. "Like what you see?" He asked with a wink as he slipped the shirt over his head.

I wiped the drool from my lips and cast my eyes down to the floor.

Ty was toying with me.

And I was angry at myself that I liked it.

Especially after just having the perfect date with Liam

last night.

Chapter 12

Once I got images of Ty wrapped in a towel out of my mind, I couldn't stop thinking about the vase full of pretty blue flowers on my desk. "How did I grow roots on the flower? I thought my magic still owed me something bad?"

Ty leaned on the table across from me as our clothes tumbled in the dryer together. "Each act must have one of equal power."

"So, repairing a ripped painting is equal to an out-of-control infection on someone's cheek?"

"To you it was. Your emotions behind the spells were of equal proportion. Your magic only judges on your desires and sacrifices, not that of anyone else's. But sometimes, magic from one spell combines with another. So, fixing the painting and your initial hex on your ex-boyfriend were both balanced with the resulting injury."

My phone beeped in my pocket. I pulled it out to see Liam's name on the screen, and I smiled.

Liam: Wanna study together tonight?

It was after lunch already and studying was my plan for the day, but Ty derailed that idea. I did want to spend some more time with Liam, but I wanted to pick Ty's brain empty of everything he knew—especially since I hadn't approached the subject of my father yet.

Ruby: I can't tonight. Tomorrow?
Liam: Sounds great. Is eight AM too early?

Ruby: No. It sounds perfect.
Liam: I'll meet you at University Grounds.

"Whatcha doing?" Ty nodded to my phone. His shiny blond hair glistened in the overhead lights. It laid neatly against his scalp and didn't fall over his face as much as it had, and I found I liked seeing his eyes. Such a vibrant shade of green.

There was no reason to lie. "Coordinating a study date for tomorrow."

Ty's mouth drooped and his eyes lost their luster. He sat back in the booth, tucking his arms under the table.

"What?" I asked, dropping my eyes to my phone. "Can't I date?"

"Date?" Ty chuckled. "I thought you were going to study."

"Well, it's both."

"Didn't you recently end your relationship with your boyfriend? Isn't he in the infirmary because you hexed him?"

"Um…" I turned my phone over in my hand. "This is someone else."

Ty shrugged, and his face went unreadable. "I was just planning on us searching for the portal tomorrow."

"It's only two o'clock right now. We can look for it as soon as my clothes are dry. That way, I'm free tomorrow to do my own things. I need to get some studying done, otherwise I'm going to fail out of school before I even begin." Ty's face crumpled as it rearranged itself, but I didn't give him time to speak. Instead, I jumped right into the information I was after. "My dad's name is Claude Warner. At least that's what he told my mom. You don't happen to know him, do you?" I held my breath for the answer. I don't know why it took me so long to ask other than fear. Fear that Ty wouldn't know him, and I'd be no closer to knowing who I was, and also fear he would. What would I do if my dad was alive? If I could find him and talk to him? What would I ask? What answers did I seek?

"Claude Warner?"

I nodded.

"Doesn't ring a bell, but you said he gave you that treasure coin?"

I nodded again.

"Your coin is from the gem dragons. I hadn't ever traveled that far south until a few weeks ago when I went hunting for their treasure."

I leaned my elbows on the table. "So, is that what you do for a living? Steal treasure? Or do you have something else more…respectable that you do?"

He laughed. "Oh, dragon hunting is respectable. Very few ever live to tell their tales, but I don't have much of a choice. I had to do something to support myself from a young age and learned quickly how to kill the dragons and take their treasure."

Kill the dragons?

I gulped at the reminder, thinking of Luke's big puppy-dog eyes.

Even if Ty had more answers for me, did I want him near me—this close to Luke?

Would Ty kill my dragon friend as soon as he ran into him?

Wasn't it only a few days ago I wished Luke would go away? My chest constricted. What if my magic brought Ty here to rid my world of Luke? And if that was the case, what was the consequence of that bit of magic?

I really didn't want Luke gone.

I couldn't believe that thought formed in my mind, but Luke had been my best friend for so many years. In fact, right now, if I didn't have Sonja, he'd be my best friend again—my only friend. I searched for words. "You *kill* the dragons? That seems a bit harsh."

He laughed. "It's the only way to get their treasure. Do you think they'd give it up willingly? In fact, if they're not dead, they'll hunt down every piece of their treasure until it's back where it belongs."

My hand reached in my pocket. Was Luke here searching for my medallion? I had left it alone in my room, and Luke didn't take it. My head was full of questions that I couldn't piece together. I plucked the first one that fluttered past. "How do you think my father ended up with a gem dragon coin?"

"He probably didn't steal it—not many men are clever enough for that." Ty smiled slyly, clearly proud of his choice of profession. "It was probably payment for services, though any smart man wouldn't take a dragon coin from a dragon that was still alive."

"Tell me more about dragons."

"Really? You know nothing about magic, yet you want to discuss dragons? Why?"

I bit my bottom lip, not wanting to give Ty any information on Luke. "They're just interesting."

"They're not that interesting. There are lots of different breeds of them, some big and some small. Some with special magical abilities, like manipulating ice or magic gems, but the only thing that interests me are their treasures."

The dryer beeped that our clothes were ready. I slipped out of the booth and filled my laundry bag, picking Ty's tunic shirt and lightweight pants out and throwing them his way. I had gotten what information I could handle from him right now. I needed to process the idea that Ty was here to hunt Luke—the thought pushed me away from Ty, despite any answers he may have.

Why was I so loyal to Luke?

I sucked in my bottom lip, remembering a day I wished I had forgotten.

I was five or so, playing in my bedroom with Luke while my mom headed to her bedroom to take a nap. She had a bottle of medicine in her hand, but I didn't think anything of it. She was sad back then, still hung up on Dad, and it was before she met her long-time boyfriend.

Luke must have sensed what she was up to. He paced outside her room. He motioned for me to go inside.

"Not now," Mom had warned. "I just need some sleep."

I heard the rattling of a bottle of pills and didn't know what it meant, but Luke did. He motioned for me to enter the room again, and I trusted him. I trusted my best friend with my whole heart. I twisted the door knob and stepped into Mom's bedroom. She had a handful of medicine in one hand and an empty bottle in the other. I didn't know what it meant until I thought about this day much later in life, but it was the first and only time Luke ever revealed himself to anyone besides me. He appeared in front of Mom. Her brown eyes grew wide as Luke's wings fluttered up, banging into her hand and knocking the pills to the ground.

"I'm going crazy," Mom said, dropping to her knees and picking up each of the pink pills.

"Do you have a headache, Mommy?"

She didn't answer. I helped her gather the capsules and handed them back to her.

"I hope you feel better, soon." I smiled.

She held her hand tight. "I will. I know I will."

Luke pushed a book across the floor with his nose. Mom didn't react, so he was back to being invisible, or she was so caught up in her own world, she didn't notice the book sliding across the floor.

"Can you read me a story?" I asked.

She nodded. Tears in her eyes.

"What's wrong?" I asked.

She shook her head. "Nothing, honey."

It wasn't until ten years later that I asked Mom about that day. She confessed to being sad and contemplating suicide. It's why she started therapy and met her ex-boyfriend, who had been her therapist.

Luke saved her life. I was sure of it.

And I should trust Luke, even now. He had warned me about Ty while in the dorm bathroom, and maybe I should have listened to Luke. Ty might have had answers for me, but I needed to be careful. I pulled out my phone and texted Liam.

Ruby: On second thought, wanna study now?
Liam: Meet you at University Grounds in fifteen.
Ruby: Perfect.

I turned towards Ty who still sat in the booth. "I'm gonna go. I really do have to study. I'm behind, and I've only had four days of classes so far."

Ty scooted out. "I thought we were going to look for

the portal."

"I don't know if that's such a great idea anymore." I shrugged and headed out of the laundromat.

"Wait," Ty called after me, but he didn't follow and I didn't stop. All I heard were his last words. "We had a deal."

We did, and I knew that. He had taught me a bit of magic. Had seemed to tell me the truth about what he did— hunt and kill dragons, but I wasn't ready for all of this. Maybe I just needed some time to process what was going on. First, I needed to find him a place to stay that wasn't right beside me in my dorm.

Maybe I just needed…something I couldn't put my finger on.

Something I had been lacking for months already.

But right now, studying sounded good.

Something normal.

And Liam seemed as normal as it got.

Chapter 13

As soon as I walked into University Grounds, Liam's smile greeted me. I pulled my backpack off my shoulder and draped it over the chair across from him. He stood and pulled me into a hug. Was it just yesterday that we had kissed? It seemed so long ago.

A day ago, I had known I was a witch, but didn't know of this whole other magical realm that existed somewhere beyond a portal. I hadn't known about dragon treasures or dragon hunters. I hadn't promised to let a dragon killer stay in my room until we found his way home.

Despite Luke's warning, I still didn't see anything threatening about Ty. He was a bit cocky and forward, but as ridiculous as it was, I found that charming.

Maybe that was enough to confirm that I should stay away. Things were going the right direction with Liam, and I didn't want to mess them up. Ty had no intentions of staying in this world and even if we were compatible, he would only bring me moments of happiness. I wanted a long-term relationship, not a one-night stand, but deep down, I know I trusted people too much. I missed my mom and craved attention.

"I thought you could use my notes. I made you copies." Liam pulled a pile of papers out of his bag and handed them to me.

"You're so sweet." I laughed. "How'd you know I was going to ask for them?"

"Call it a hunch."

"Thanks for the help."

"I can't let my girl fail out of school."

My chest constricted. "Your girl?" We had only had one real date. I didn't count the first time we met at the coffee shop or when I bailed on him at Young Monsters. Maybe this is what being grown up was like? You didn't play games and just said what was on your mind. Ty certainly had done that, and I found it refreshing.

Liam looked down and pulled something out of his bag. It was brown with long, thin leather straps. "At least I was hoping you'd be my girl." He held out the object in his hand. It was a leather bracelet that tied on a wrist, a little over an inch thick. There was a single, multi-color stone in the center. "I brought this for you."

Was he moving too fast?

My thoughts must have been clear on my face, because he laughed. "It doesn't have to mean anything. I just wanted you to have it. I saw it this morning and wanted to get it for you."

I shook my head. I had just been drooling over another man who I had seen almost naked. Who killed dragons. I was still letting that fact settle in. "I'm sorry, but I can't take it."

Liam shrugged. "Ruby, I got it just for you. It doesn't mean anything other than a symbol of our new friendship." He urged it to me. "Would you refuse a gift from a friend?"

I sighed as I looked at the colors swirling in the stone. It looked like an opal. Would I refuse a gift from Sonja? No, of course not. It'd be rude.

He continued to persuade me. "It's just costume jewelry. I thought it was nice and nerdy and you'd love it."

Now he had me smiling. It was nice and nerdy, and I did love it. I swallowed my pride and took it from him.

"Here, let me help you." He tied it onto my wrist, and I fell in love—with the jewelry, not Liam—though, I could see how that might be easy to do. I turned my wrist, catching the glint of the lights off the stone. Costume jewelry or not, it was beautiful.

I hugged Liam. "Thank you. It's a nice gift. First flowers, then jewelry, what other surprises do you have for me?"

"I can't tell you. They wouldn't be surprises then." His chair screeched against the tile floor as he pulled it out, and we sat down together. "I could start by explaining my notes."

I nodded. Right. We were here to study. I scooted around the table to sit right next to him, the warmth of his body radiating into me. Studying. Sure. That didn't sound as fun as kissing him. I positioned my bracelet wearing wrist on the table and kept glancing down at his gift as he went through his notes.

Half an hour into the session, I rubbed my eyes. I wasn't cut out for economics, that was for sure. Perhaps I could still drop the class and get a full refund. "I need a mocha. Want anything?"

Liam stood, pulling a wallet from his back pocket. "I'm sorry. I should have offered as soon as you came in. I'll get it."

I nodded and sat back down, staring out the window by our table.

There, out on the sidewalk, my friend Luke sat on top of a blue post office box. He stared at me through the window, and when he was sure he had my attention, he shook his head at me like he had in my dorm's shower room.

But Ty wasn't here. Did Luke not want me spending time with any men? I rubbed my face. When I was younger, it was like Luke and I had this mental connection where we didn't have to speak. We knew what each other was trying to say without a word.

Now, we were strangers. Lost best friends that couldn't quite reconnect. Where was that dragon that had made me laugh a few days ago on the dance floor? Something had changed. He wanted something, and it was up to me to figure out what he needed.

"Liam," I flagged his attention from the line. "I'll be right back. I need to take care of something."

Liam tilted his chin, but I didn't think he needed an explanation. The bells on the coffee shop door jingled as I stepped onto the sidewalk, but there was no golden dragon on top of the mailbox. No signs of Luke at all.

As I headed back inside by Liam, my stomach twisted. Why didn't Luke want me with Ty or Liam? Maybe something else made Luke uneasy. I wish I trusted Ty enough to discuss Luke with him, since he was the only person who would understand. Ty was a dragon hunter. He killed dragons. Could I make him promise not to go after Luke and trust that he would keep his word?

I didn't know him well enough. If I spent more time with him, I'd get a better feel for his trustworthiness.

Plus, Ty was the closest I had been to figuring out how to control my magic.

And right now, I wanted that more than anything.

Then why was I here with Liam?

Liam joined me with my mocha, and I slurped off the whipped cream. "Thank you," I said.

Liam laughed, reaching out a finger and wiping cream from my lip. My heart pitter-pattered at the touch, and I remembered why I was here. Liam made me feel special in a way Geoff never did.

Is this what adults did? Balance multiple relationships at once? It'd only been a day or two and I was already drained. I was looking for a long-term, stable relationship with Liam, but I wasn't ready to move as quickly as he was moving. With Ty, I only wanted answers…and maybe another glimpse of him shirtless.

Confused was an understatement, but why did I need to make any decisions?

Nobody was asking me to.

Either way, I needed to study and I might as well have Liam as company…he did just give me a beautiful gift. I twisted my wrist and admired the stone again, knowing it was my turn to do something nice for him next.

Chapter 14

My study date with Liam ended abruptly in a quick kiss and an "I'll see you at school on Monday." I thought I had done something wrong, but he had said he hoped I enjoyed my present.

As I climbed my dorm stairs up to the seventh floor, I expected to see Ty leaning lazily against my door. I ran through all the ways to get out of letting him stay in my room. It was against the rules. If I got caught, I could be kicked out of Einstein Hall. When I made him that promise, I was desperate for information. Now that I had received some of what I wanted, was I hypocritical that I wanted out of our agreement?

Yup. Call me hypocritical.

As I headed down the empty hallway, my heart sank while I pulled my keys out to unlock my room. Ty wasn't there. I glanced over my shoulder as I stepped inside, but there was no sign of anyone out in the halls, much less the man who confused me.

Inside my room, I was greeted by Luke with his wings flapping and tail wagging. I laughed. "So, are you going to tell me why you don't like the boys who I spend time with?"

Luke shook his head side to side.

Hmm, did he understand my question? I thought his movements had been coincidental, but maybe there was more going on in that little dragon head than I thought.

"Do you like me?" I asked.

Luke eagerly shook his head up and down. I had thought that the way Luke and I communicated when I was a child had been all in my mind, but maybe there was something to it.

"Do you like Liam?"

Another shake no.

"How about Ty?"

No again.

"Is it because he's a dragon hunter?"

Luke shook his head yes.

Interesting. I hopped on my bed and pulled my mom's painting from the top of my bookshelf. "Do you know about magic?"

The dragon shook his head. So much for that. One last try. I pulled out my coin and asked, "Is this yours?"

The dragon nodded.

"How did my dad get it?"

Luke flew up onto my bed and took the coin in his mouth. He flew to my jewelry box and lifted the lid with a clawed foot, tossing the coin inside. That wasn't an answer. I rubbed my temple. Luke may be a magical creature, but he wasn't a magic eight ball. There was only so much he knew and could communicate. Luke shut the jewelry box lid, causing the flowers in the vase beside it to shake. The little blue flowers were growing vigorously. The entire vase was filled with roots and a few grew up, escaping the top of the glass. The other flowers were shriveled to nothingness.

Ty had taught me something that appeared to be working. I glanced at the bag of Geoff's things by my door, and my skin turned to ice knowing what I had to do. Even with one less outfit inside, I needed to return them to their owner and check on Geoff's skin condition in the process. I hadn't confirmed the magic balancing tip Ty had taught me had worked.

I yawned and changed into a baggy sleepy kitty t-shirt

and matching boxer shorts, then crawled into bed. In the morning I'd head over to Geoff's dorm. If he was doing well, he'd be downstairs in the fitness room, like he was every Sunday morning.

If he was still injured—well, he might not be home at all.

* * *

The next morning at about nine, I headed out of my dorm carrying the bag of Geoff's things and trudged a few blocks down to his dorm. Through the window on the street, I could see a few people in the fitness center. My eyes darted from a tall, fit woman on a treadmill to two scrawny kids trying to lift weights and settled on an older gentleman who was wiping down a butterfly machine. No Geoff.

Maybe he still was ill.

I swallowed a lump as I headed inside. As I crossed the lobby to the main desk area, I heard feminine giggling from the lounge. I turned around to see Geoff, dressed in his workout clothing, nuzzling the redhead's neck. My shoulders tensed and the bag of Geoff's things crumpled in my grip.

I wanted to run away and hide before Geoff noticed me, but that was the old Ruby. This one would accomplish what she came here to do. She had control of her magic, she might already have a new boyfriend, and she was going to make sure she got an "A" in economics.

Take that Geoff.

I cleared my throat and stood tall, lifting my chin while approaching my ex. His eyes rolled up to see me standing beside him, but he didn't move his lips from Red's neck, but I got my confirmation—his cheek was perfectly smooth.

There was my proof my magic was under control—thanks to Ty.

How much more could he help me with?

I'd never know if I chased him away. My stomach turned. Had I been that rude to Ty as I zipped out of the laundromat to meet Liam?

I held out the bag of Geoff's clothes and cleared my throat. "I brought your things back."

He pulled away from Red's neck and sat back on the sofa, pulling the girl into his side. "It's junk. I don't need it." There was no emotion in his words, and they tore my heart in half. After three years, all I saw was coldness. He turned his shoulder to me and licked Red's neck, making her giggle.

He was mean. He deserved the skin condition.

But he had never been like this. Was he getting back at me for my little show with Liam at the coffee shop? Maybe I had misread his actions with Red back then and hurt him?

My hands fisted, and I dropped the bag and turned to leave.

But I stopped. The bag of items were junk? Well, I knew someone who could use them. I snatched the clothes and headed back to Einstein hall. My feet wanted to slam into the pavement in an all-out sprint, but I kept my emotions in check. I wouldn't give Geoff the satisfaction.

It was a good thing I didn't have my medallion along, or Geoff may not have recovered from what I hexed him with this time.

I took my dorm's stairs two-by-two and my lungs burned when I arrived on the seventh floor. I marched down the hallway, ignoring the tears that finally broke free.

Why wasn't I over Geoff? He was an ass.

And the way he was treating me made me feel like an ass, too.

Was he really that bitter with me that he deliberately had to do things to make me mad?

At the end of the hallway, leaning lazily against my door, just as I had pictured him yesterday was Ty. I wiped my tears on my sleeve, not wanting him to see me like this. When they wouldn't stop, I pushed forward anyway. The comfort of my room was more important than my pride right now.

I pulled my keys from my pocket and thought about economics. About pizza. About my date with Liam. Anything to make my eyes dry up.

But nothing worked.

As I approached the door, trying to see clear enough to get the key into the lock, Ty's fresh scent enveloped me as he leaned close, almost wrapping me in a hug, yet not touching me. His words were soft in a way that I didn't expect. "Hey, what happened? What's wrong?"

Chapter 15

"Nothing's wrong," I turned my head away from Ty as more tears threatened to fall from my stinging eyes. I shoved Geoff's bag of things into Ty's arms. "These are all for you." I fumbled with my keys and unlocked my dorm room.

Inside, I plopped down at my desk chair with my back to Ty and pulled out the medallion from my jewelry box. Could I do some magic to make me no longer care about how stupid I had been to give three years of my life to that asshat? And stupid I didn't realize he had been distant the past year. I had been so preoccupied that I didn't pay attention to his behaviors. Thinking back, now I saw how we didn't go out anymore, how he spent more and more time with his football friends while I played nurse to Mom.

Sure, it was nice to have someone to help me when I needed it, but if I would have dumped him sophomore year and chosen to date my costar in the school play instead, would I be in a different place right now?

I wouldn't have moved out here to Bloomington.

I would be at home, in that Victorian house where I belonged.

I would have made my mom go in for routine doctor visits.

The door behind me clicked shut, and Ty's soft breathing filled the silent room.

"Can magic change the past?" My voice cracked, but I didn't care. I wanted to know that answer.

Ty's words were filled with something I didn't comprehend. Remorse maybe? "No. What's done is done."

It was for the best. I placed my hand over my long-sleeve t-shirt where Liam's bracelet was tightly fastened on my wrist. If I hadn't dated Geoff, I wouldn't have found Liam. He would have had no reason to kiss me at the coffee shop, sending whatever dominoes brought us together toppling over. Everything was for the best. I just needed to get through my emotions right now.

"Why are you here?" I snapped as I spun around to face Ty, not expecting the harshness that sprang from my throat.

Ty ground his teeth, allowing a muscle to twitch in his jaw. "You promised to help me look for the portal."

I softened my tone. "I did, but I can't today."

Ty circled around me, sitting on my bed beside my desk. His jaw still tense, but he shrugged like he didn't have a care in the world. "The longer you wait to help me, the longer you have a roommate." He undid his boots and crawled back onto my bed, leaning against my pillow. He crossed his arms over his chest and shot me the smuggest smile.

"I can get dorm security up here in minutes." I don't know why I said it, because I had no plans on getting rid of Ty. He held the answers I had been searching for the past months, or maybe for my entire life.

And Ty knew it. He snuggled into the pillow and closed his eyes. "You have a lot to learn from me yet. It'd be a shame to pass up the opportunity."

He was right.

And I hated him for it. The more I knew Ty, the more he seemed to bring the worst out of me, or maybe he brought the real Ruby out. The one I hid from others, trying to be the perfect student, girlfriend, and daughter. Did Ty purposely push my buttons like Geoff was doing? Was it fun to aggravate me? As soon as I thought those words, I knew the answer. Yes, it was. Sonja always laughed at my extreme facial expressions, saying I shouted my mood without saying a word. Well, it was time to get a handle on that.

Ty opened one eye and lifted his head, taking a good look at me, then he laughed. "The sooner you help me find the portal, the sooner I'll return home."

I leaned back in my chair, defeated. Why was I being so rude? Ty had honestly done nothing wrong. I blew out a breath. "I'm not mad at you."

"You could have fooled me."

I wanted to explain what I had just seen with Geoff, but Ty didn't need to hear about my boy trouble. Instead, I gave him my surrender. "I'm not mad at you at all. I'm all yours." Ty perked up, flashing a slightly naughty eyebrow arch, so I clarified to stop whatever he was thinking. "I mean, how do we go about finding this portal?"

With a large, boyish smile, Ty maneuvered to the foot of the bed, only a foot or two from where I sat. "You use your magic to locate it."

I opened my jewelry box and pulled out my medallion. "What would be the balance of finding a portal?"

"It's not that easy. Portals don't want to be found, and you can't use that kind of magic to locate them. You need to be in close enough proximity to one, and then…sense it."

I leaned back in my chair, nearly toppling it over. "Then why do you need me? Can't you just roam around town until you sense it?"

Ty pushed his hair behind his ears. "It's not that easy. Remember what I said about not being magical? Well, only a magical being—like a witch—can feel a portal's presence.

Plus, you need magic to see it."

I rubbed my temple. "So, I just wish to see the portal?"

"You wish for magic sight—which allows you to identify all things magical."

"But to do this, I need to balance the magic. I need to sacrifice something?"

Ty nodded. "You're getting the hang of things. Your sacrifice needs to be of equal weight to keep the balance. Magic must be neutral. So, an act that will bring you a gain will need to be balanced with an act that is a loss."

"Like, if I give up my sense of taste, I can balance the sense of magic sight?"

"Do you think those two senses are equal? Vision and taste? If not, you should always over sacrifice to prevent things from going wrong. Like, maybe give up your sense of taste and your sense of hearing."

My mouth went dry, picturing a world without both taste and hearing.

Ty waved his hand. "Of course, it's only temporary while we search for the portal. You can make another sacrifice to return to normal once we're done looking for the day."

Temporary, huh? I could handle that. I clutched the medallion. "Do I have to *wish* for my vision to change? It seems like it should come a different way."

"Wishing seems to be the easiest way for baby witches to channel their power, in conjunction with a magic object— your coin, for instance. Older and more powerful witches don't need to do either." Ty smiled, and I wanted to smack him for comparing me to a baby.

"I got it." I rubbed the medallion between my fingers, searching for speckles of magic and sending them to my eyes.

Magic sight. Then I sent my taste and my hearing to the medallion in exchange.

The world went silent. I opened my eyes to Ty laying back in my bed again with his arms folded behind his head.

A golden glow illuminated from the pale skin of my hands. I pulled up one leg of my jeans to see my legs glowing as well. In the mirror, my face shimmered like the rest of me. Magic sight. I was magical, so I glowed. Simple as that. Ty on the other hand, appeared no different than before.

In my palm, my medallion had a radiance as well, but nothing else in the room seemed any different.

That was until Ty sat up. His lips were moving, but I didn't hear anything. A dim glow peeked through the fabric of Ty's shirt in the center of his chest. I stood and crossed the few feet between us, touching the spot right over his breast bone. Ty scooted away, shaking his head, but I moved closer, backing him up to the wall my bed was pushed against. Beneath his tunic shirt was a lump.

"What is this?" I asked.

Ty covered his ears. His lips moved again, but I didn't hear what he was saying.

"What?" I asked.

He moved his lips again, and I tried to make out his words. "You. Don't. Have. To. Yell."

Was I yelling? I couldn't tell. My world was dead silent. I tried to whisper. "What is this?"

Ty pulled a leather string out from under his shirt, showing me the necklace I had seen while he had showered yesterday, but I hadn't paid much attention then. My eyes were on...other things. The leather tie looped around a polished stone pendant. A jade-colored circle with a hole in the middle.

Ty's lips moved, but I missed most his words. The only one I made out was, "Mother."

I suddenly felt vulnerable, realizing what I had done. I was standing in my room without a sense of taste or hearing with a man I barely knew. Ty could be anyone or this could just be a step he was taking in his dragon hunting adventure. A way to find Luke.

But if Ty was honest about magic vision finding a portal to get him home as quickly as possible, trusting him may be best for Luke as well. I just needed to pump him for as much information as possible while he was here. Too bad that was nearly impossible while I couldn't hear.

I just nodded and smiled at whatever he was saying. I'd ask him about his necklace and the world he came from after we looked for the portal today.

"Ready?" I said a bit louder than a whisper. Hopefully, I had hit the right volume. When Ty smiled and slipped his feet back into his boots, I knew I got it right.

"After you," he mouthed—or said. He gave an old-fashioned bow towards the door.

"Where are we going?"

His mouth moved again, but I just shrugged, not catching his words. Who knew hearing was so important?

He shook his head and rubbed a hand through his hair. "Follow me." He took my hand, not giving me a chance to refuse.

I glanced at his hand, noticing the scars between his fingers. Instead of pulling away, I brushed my fingers along the old wounds, feeling their roughness. Ty had lived a hard life, and yet, he was playful and full of energy. Maybe finding this portal would be a fun adventure after all.

I wrapped my fingers around his hand, strangely excited for his touch—strictly as friends, of course—and gave him a nod to go ahead, following him out of the dorm.

Chapter 16

It wasn't until Ty led me past University Grounds Coffee Haus that I started to worry we'd run into Liam. What would he think if he saw me holding hands with another man? It wasn't like I could explain that I was helping Ty find a magical portal. And how would I even make up an excuse about what was going on without my hearing?

I knew I should drop Ty's hand. I wasn't blind. I just couldn't hear if someone was saying, "Excuse me," while they tried to pass me on the busy sidewalk or if someone yelled for me to get out of the way, not that that happened often. Ty's hand provided me with a safety net in this unknown world.

Ty must have sensed my trepidation. He pulled me out of the flow of foot traffic and tried saying something, but I couldn't read his rapid lips. My heart raced as people passed us, and I pulled my hand out of his. This was insane. Ty's eyebrows knitted together, and his lips tightened. "Go home?" he mouthed.

Yes. Back to the safety of my dorm where I could wish for my hearing back and there was no chance that I'd run into my new boyfriend and blow our relationship before it even got started, but I shook my head, "No," instead. I wouldn't go back on my word for a second time. If I couldn't be brave enough to make it five blocks away from my dorm, I shouldn't be away at college.

I twisted around for a glimpse through University Grounds' front window. Nobody inside resembled Liam, so I took a deep breath and took Ty's hand again. The familiarity of it sent an excited shiver up my arm, but I ignored the sensation and gave Ty a nod. "I'm good. Let's go."

His eyes were cast down at our intertwined fingers. Did he feel the same comfort I felt? Before I could assess his face, he spun around and led me off campus grounds to a different part of the city. He pulled me into an empty bus stop, and we sat on the bench inside. Ty dropped my hand, and it felt cold. I rubbed it.

He lifted my chin so my eyes found his lips. "Do you see anything here?" He spoke slowly, allowing me to piece together his words.

Everything seemed normal. Cars passing on the street in front of a restaurant, biker bar, and tattoo parlor across the road. Nothing with a soft golden glow…or any glow at all. "Nothing unusual."

"Okay," Ty mouthed. "Hold your coin."

I pulled the dragon medallion from my pocket and gripped it in my hand.

My eyes returned to Ty's lips. "Feel… magic. Feel…magic somewhere else…"

I hadn't caught all his words. "I don't know what you mean."

Ty covered my hand with his, and I looked down to our hands. They fit together well, and I wanted to lean against his side. What was I doing? Ty's finger touched my chin and tilted my head up to look at his lips again. "Feel the warmth?"

I nodded.

"That's magic."

I sucked in my bottom lip and waited for his next instructions. As I stared at his lips, I noticed a fine scar through his top lip. What caused that? Dragon hunting? Despite his athletic physique and his battle wounds, I still couldn't picture him killing a dragon such as Luke. Ty had shown me only gentleness and compassion, not what I expected of a killer. Maybe my thoughts were nothing more than wishful thinking.

Ty's lips moved again, saying each word slowly to give me time to follow along. "Feel for the warmth from somewhere outside you. What direction is the warmest?"

I felt like a goof, staring so intently at his mouth, but I didn't know what else to do. I looked up into his eyes. They darted back and forth slightly, as he seemed to take in my entire face.

"Close your eyes and feel."

He was right. I had too many distractions. My brain was going through all sorts of things except finding this portal. As I closed my eyes, my heart raced at the complete lack of sensation. Without hearing or sight, sitting at a bus stop was a bit unnerving. I fluttered my eyes open.

"I'm here." Ty must have seen the fear on my face. "It's okay." He must have thought that I was the biggest scaredy cat.

I took a deep breath and closed my eyes again. Forgetting about the dirty bus stop where I was sitting. Forgetting about how close Ty was and how his comforting hand was still on mine. Forgetting about everything other than finding which direction was the warmest. I focused on the skin on my face. My forehead, each cheek, and my chin, but each part seemed to be the same temperature.

I opened my eyes briefly and stood, taking Ty to his feet beside me. Once again, I closed my eyes, and dropped Ty's hand to slowly turn in a circle. As I spun, a slight warmth appeared on my cheek, and as I continued on my path, the warmth moved across my face. It was like I was standing a few feet from a campfire on a cool night, and as I turned, the warmth caressed my body. I waited until the sensation was flat upon my face, covering it equally before I opened my eyes.

"That way." I pointed towards Kirkwood Avenue—the main vintage shopping area of town.

Ty smiled and pulled me in for a hug, trapping me in his strong arms and against his comforting body, but I stiffened.

His chest vibrated against my face, but he loosened up. He patted me on the back. "Suck it up. It was only a hug," he mouthed.

With my hand back in his, Ty lead me onto the main road, and we headed in the direction of the magic.

Fifteen minutes later, we were at the start of the business district on Kirkwood. The first shop sold vintage clothing. Ty pointed to his eyes, then to the store.

"Yeah, I know. Magic portal."

He shushed me with a finger to his lips. Perhaps I had said that a bit loudly. We climbed the three steps into the cozy little shop that smelled of old people—stale and a bit like moth balls. The racks overflowed with clothing, but nothing stood out. Ty led me through the store, and in a minute or two, we had traveled through every room and down every aisle. Before pulling me out of the building, Ty picked up a sombrero with a giant rainbow ribbon around the rim. He put it on and did a little dance that was way more country in style than fit the hat.

I laughed out loud.

Where had that come from? He reminded me a bit of Luke. Goofy and just enjoying life.

Before I was even done laughing, Ty had the hat back on the rack and we were out the door and on our way into an antique shop next door.

We repeated our quick search of the aisles, but as we stepped into a back room about the size of a small bedroom, I stopped at a familiar golden glow.

I maneuvered around an aisle of silver serving dishes to a little statue of a dragon shimmering with magic.

This dragon didn't look at all like Luke. It had three heads, ferocious teeth, and sharp claws that I could imagine tearing those large marks into Ty's chest.

I lifted it, feeling the warmth in my hand.

"What is this?" I asked Ty.

He shrugged. "Just a trinket."

I leaned in and whispered. "It glows."

He shook his head, mouthing something like, "It's not important. Many items have spells on them."

I shook my head, fanning my hand around the building with thousands of trinkets—all of them lacking the luster of this one.

I looked at the price: nineteen dollars. I'd gladly part with that much money to learn more. I led Ty to the cashier and paid for my item. Soon, it was wrapped and in a little bag.

Ty and I continued our perusal of the stores along Kirkwood, but didn't find any portals. As the day went on, Ty grew goofier and goofier, as if he was intentionally trying to make me laugh—and it worked. I don't remember the last time I had such a good time. It definitely was before my mom passed away.

When we ran into a pawn shop, Ty turned one of his dragon coins—which did not glow—into twenty bucks and bought us a bag of cotton candy with money to spare at a stand outside one of the stores. It wasn't until I took the first bite that

I realized I couldn't taste it, but that was okay. The look on Ty's face while enjoying the fluffy mess of sugar—probably for the first time in his life—was enough. What was Ty's realm like? Did he love it there? Finding the portal was important to him, so my guess was he did like his world. How could he not? It was home.

I asked him questions about his world, but it was hard to understand everything without my hearing. I caught enough details to know it was like the middle-ages...but with dragons and other magical creatures. I'd have to ask more when I could hear what he was saying.

Even though we didn't find Ty's way home, the day was...well...unexpectedly fun.

Until we ran into Liam.

I spotted him first, thank goodness, and dropped Ty's hand before Liam lifted his head from his book and found me standing with a half-eaten bag of cotton candy. A huge smile grew on Liam's face and I tried to match it, but the panic in my chest probably made me look surprised rather than happy. Before Liam was in earshot, I filled Ty in. "That's...Liam. I'm kinda...dating him. He gave me the flowers."

A look of understanding fell on Ty's face, and he didn't go for my hand again. I pulled my medallion from my pocket and tugged at its magic, attempting to sacrifice my magic sight so I could hear normally, but I didn't have enough time. Liam was right in front of me.

"Liam!" I said. "I didn't expect to see you here."

He nodded towards the antique store we had gone through earlier that day. I fixed my eyes to his lips, trying to keep on top of the conversation. Luckily, Ty gave me lots of practice reading lips today. "I live down here. Above that shop over there." Okay, that wasn't exactly what he said, but I pieced together the one or two words I got along with his actions to figure out what he was trying to say.

"It must be fun to be where all the action is."

"It's a bit distracting..." I missed the rest of his words, but when his eyes raked over Ty and asked the next question, I was back in the conversation. "Who's your friend?"

My friend? I tried to piece together a story about how I let this man I just met lead me all around the city holding my hand...and that he was staying at my place. I looked to Ty, but saw his lips already moving. He came to my rescue.

"My name's Ty. I'm her cousin and just popped in to visit."

Liam extended his hand. "Nice to meet you."

Ty nodded and gave it a shake.

I needed out of here before I had to explain why I couldn't hear the conversation. "It's getting dark, and we still need to walk home. I'll see you at school tomorrow?"

"You bet." Liam pulled me into a hug, and his chest vibrated from words, but I couldn't see his lips. When he stopped talking and kissed my cheek. I couldn't help but notice Ty averting his eyes at the tiny display of affection, but it was too late. I saw jealousy on his face. I scooted out of Liam's arms and waved goodbye—in the cutest way I could.

Our walk home was uneventful, but the setting sun filled the sky with reds and pinks, causing a soft melancholy atmosphere. I didn't need to hold his hand, since I knew the route well and the crowds had settled down, but a few times, my hand had a mind of its own and I had to fight to keep it to myself. After hours today of walking around the city hand in hand, it was a sensation that was hard to break.

The whole way home I was sad to see the day end, but then remembered Ty was staying with me. We walked up the stairs together, and I unlocked my dorm room. It only seemed right to end the night, before we started the next chapter in my room—where I'd use my magic to return my senses back to normal.

"I had a nice time," I said with my eyes fixed on Ty's lips.

He smiled. "I wish we found the portal."

And that quickly, I returned to reality. Today was nothing more than Ty looking for a way home. He wouldn't be here much longer if we succeeded, and there was no point in making friends. I smiled and led him into my dorm.

I sat down, and rubbed my medallion in my hand, wishing to give up the magic sight, and have my sense of taste and touch back.

The medallion warmed, and when I opened my eyes, Ty's lips moved, but I didn't hear anything. I tried again, really digging deep, but again, nothing happened.

I tried again, thinking of a new sacrifice. Return my senses back to normal, and I'd skip breakfast for the entire week...and I loved breakfast.

My world stayed silent. "It's not working."

Ty covered his ears. I must have yelled again.

What if my senses never returned?

My heart raced, and I breathed rapidly. I didn't know enough about this magic stuff, and I was trusting a guy I barely knew to teach me? A guy who couldn't do magic himself?

What if my sacrifice just wasn't big enough? I closed my eyes again and wished for my hearing and normal sight, telling the magic it could keep my taste—for now.

Still nothing.

I couldn't go on without hearing. Yes, magic sight was useful, but hearing was critical for my life...at least right now with attending college.

Ty dropped to his knees in front of me, putting his hand on my chin and causing me to watch his lips again. "Calm down. It's okay. Try again, but slower and more direct."

I nodded. I closed my eyes, pulled the magic from the medallion, and made my wish, as clear and deliberate as possible. I pulled at every piece of magic I recognized inside me and focused on my eyes, ears, and tongue.

The warmth of the medallion increased and when I opened my eyes, my body didn't glow anymore. "Say something." I demanded of Ty.

"You sure panic a lot."

My hearing was back. "You sure don't know how to say anything nice, do you?" I teased. I had one more sense I needed to confirm was back to normal—my sense of taste.

My first thought was to kiss Ty. What would he taste like?

I laughed at myself and shooed that thought away. Instead, I pushed my sleeve up and licked my arm. Yuck. Salty.

When I looked up, I expected a sarcastic comment from Ty, but instead, he focused on my bracelet with the most serious expression I had ever seen on him. "Where did you get that?"

Why did he care? I saw how he looked at Liam and me today, I didn't need to add more fuel to the fire. "It's not important."

"No really. Where did you get it?"

His insistence hit a nerve, and I didn't want to admit Liam gave it to me. It made our relationship seem so serious, when it was nothing more than a few dates. "Why does it matter to you?"

He gritted his teeth and kicked off his boots. "I guess it doesn't matter. I'm calling dibs on the bed."

All the fun we had earlier today was quickly forgotten. Ty was back to getting under my skin. "That wasn't the deal."

Ty laid back on my pillow and tucked his arms beneath his head. "Then you'll have to sleep beside me."

I sucked in my bottom lip. He was intentionally trying to piss me off. What other explanation was there for his ability to ruin a nearly perfect day with only a few words?

I wasn't going to let him win. I took my sleepy kitty t-shirt, bedtime shorts, bathroom bag and headed down the hall to change. When I returned to my dorm, I plopped into my little twin sized bed right beside Ty. Ha. I bet he didn't expect that.

"You should know that I snore," I said, turning over and flicking off the light.

Chapter 17

I awoke way too late the next morning with a pounding heart, but, oddly, it wasn't from the man beside me in bed. I was going to be late for school.

Falling asleep gave me trouble last night with Ty beside me—not because of anything other than my imagination going wild. Everything about him irritated me, from how he took up more than half the bed to how he smelled like a fall thunderstorm, from how his warmth made me want to cuddle up at his side to the fact that he didn't seem to have any trouble sleeping.

As I rushed into economics, my heart nearly stopped at the sight of Liam. My cheeks heated, thinking about how I woke up beside another man.

Not that it meant anything, but it didn't look good.

Liam and I weren't exclusively dating, were we? My hand rubbed the bracelet on my wrist. Perhaps we were.

I took a deep breath as I walked the steps along the perimeter of the lecture hall, hoping the professor didn't notice me slipping in. As he turned his head my way, I reached for a bit of magic and created a balance. Urging him to look at Geoff instead of me, and I'd forgo one correct answer on the next quiz as payment. My medallion grew warm, and I smiled.

This magic stuff was going to be a lot of fun.

"Ruby, so nice of you to join us."

My heart leapt in my throat. He wasn't supposed to notice me. Perhaps he spotted me before I cast the spell. My cheeks grew uncomfortably hot as I hurried down to my seat and slipped beside Liam.

He leaned towards me and whispered, "I was worried about you."

I smiled. "I'm fine. Just overslept."

"Did your cousin keep you out late?"

"No. We…went to bed as soon as we got home." That didn't sound good, but before I could further explain, the professor shot me a glare. I bit down on my words and focused towards the front of the classroom. It'd have to wait.

Class dragged on, and I cursed Geoff for convincing me that every career was built off economics…even if this class did bring Liam and I together. And I met Kat. I glanced behind me, but she wasn't there.

"She dropped out," Liam whispered.

My stomach sank. I hadn't even had the chance to get to know her yet. "She dropped out? Like of this class or of college?"

"College."

There went my optimism about a friend here in Bloomington that wasn't male. I hoped everything was okay. A hollowness settled inside me. Should I take what happened to Kat as a warning? If I kept not focusing on my studies, would I be forced to drop out, too? Or worse…get *kicked* out?

When the clock ticked away the final minutes of class and the professor gave us our reading assignment, Liam turned towards me. "Wanna get some pizza tonight?" His eyes glanced down at my wrist. I nonchalantly pushed my shirt sleeve up to show that I was wearing his bracelet. Yup, maybe we were an item.

"Pizza would be great." I needed time away from Ty, anyway. "As long as we can get some studying done."

"We could order delivery and hit the books. I could

meet you at your place."

My mouth went dry. Was Ty still in my room? I shook my head. "I haven't cleaned. How about yours?"

Liam shook his head. "Roommates. We'll just meet down at Pie-R-Squared. They have a big back room we can study in."

I nodded; happy I dodged that one.

As I headed into the hallway, my thoughts hung on why my magic didn't work to prevent the professor noticing I was late for class. Surely, sacrificing a quiz answer was more than enough to keep the balance. Last night, my magic had hesitated as well. I rubbed my temple. Just when I thought I was getting the hang of using my gift, it reverted to being sporadic like when my mom first told me I was one-quarter witch.

Could I confirm it was on the fritz?

I needed to try a small and simple spell. Stopping at a piece of gum stuck to the floor, I pulled my medallion out of my pocket and fisted it in the palm of my hand. I didn't really care about the gum stuck to the floor, so this shouldn't take much of a sacrifice. I channeled my magic through the medallion and through me, wishing for the gum to be off the floor and stuck to the wall instead. In exchange, I offered up the fresh pack of gum I had in the bottom of my bag.

Nothing happened. Nothing at all.

I tried again, waiting until the medallion warmed in my hand, but this time, it didn't warm any more than from my own body heat.

Maybe the medallion was faulty. Maybe I had one of Ty's coins instead, but when I examined the writing on the back of the piece of silver, I knew it was mine.

What was going on?

I needed Ty.

A laugh rolled from my lips at the absurd thought…but it was true.

Leaving the gum behind, I forced myself to sit through my next class, and during my hour break for lunch, I headed back to my dorm.

Once home, I flung my room's door open to an empty room.

"Urgh!" Of course. When I needed him, he was nowhere to be found.

I shoved a piece of beef jerky into my mouth and headed back to the main campus for my next class. As soon as I made it out onto the sidewalk, a familiar friend began to skip beside me. His wings flapped, tail wagged, and even a little smoke escaped his over-sized nostrils. My buddy Luke was back.

After about half a block, my anger and anxiety disappeared, and I laughed. I loved his child-like innocence. Luke walked with me all the way to my next class and danced on stage while the professor lectured. He then crawled across a few students' desks, making them drop their books, notes, or pencils like a gust of wind had swept through the lecture hall.

By the end of class, I was feeling better. I'd find Ty, and he'd tell me what was going on, but for now, I had two more classes to get through before my date with Liam.

And I was looking forward to it. I didn't need any magic when I was with him. He liked me for who I was…unlike Ty who only wanted me to help him find something.

Luke came racing down the aisle and crawled down by my feet, and I laughed.

No matter what happened with Liam or Ty, I had my dragon. He was my best friend who more than liked me—he was completely loyal and faithful to me. Everything was going to be fine.

* * *

My pizza study date went well with Liam. He walked me home, but I didn't invite him up because I was worried that Ty was upstairs, sprawled out in my bed. Instead, right outside the glass entry door, Liam brushed the hair off my face and pressed his lips to mine. His entire body leaned against me while one hand rested on my hip while the other wrapped around my back.

"Maybe we could plan for me to come upstairs one day soon?" He pulled away breathless, and I knew what he was after.

I wasn't ready for what Liam was asking, and it was good I was worried Ty was upstairs. How far would Liam and I have gone if I didn't have a reason to keep him outside?

"Maybe one day soon," I left the sentence vague as I headed inside.

Where I almost slammed into Ty in the lobby.

"What are you doing here?" I snapped.

"Watching your little lip-to-lip session."

My heart was like thunder booming in my chest. Why did I feel like I was in trouble? "Obviously. That's none of your business."

Ty shrugged. "Maybe not, but it's kinda fun to watch." I stopped. "What?"

"It's kinda like when you see something bad, you can't

stop looking at it."

My hands tightened into fists, and I turned my back to him, taking the steps two-by-two back to my dorm. I knew he said things like that just to push my buttons. He got a kick out of aggravating me. How did I ever think he was kind and sweet? Perhaps I *could* see him out hunting dragons and ramming some archaic weapon through their scales.

I needed to be careful. I wouldn't let him get to me, but a snarky comment formed in my mind, and I couldn't resist as we hiked up the steps. "I think you couldn't stop watching us outside because you wished that it was you kissing me."

He laughed. "And what if I did wish that?"

I stopped and turned around to see Ty's expression, to read what I couldn't tell from the tone of his voice. He was close on my heels, and as soon as I hesitated, he zipped past me, hiding his face. I waited to catch my breath and get some distance between us. No matter how good of shape I was in, stairs always left me winded. Sure, there was an elevator, but it was impossibly slow and this was the only exercise in my life, so I promised myself I'd always take the stairs.

Ty met me outside my dorm, where he relaxed against my door, seemingly unaffected by both my previous comment and the steps we just hiked up. He played with a scar on his hand and didn't look at me like he usually did. I let the conversation drop. "Any luck with the portal today?"

He shook his head, causing his blond hair to loosen from behind his ears. "No. I was hoping we were going to do that tonight, but you didn't come home."

"I had a date."

One corner of his lips turned up into a smile. "I saw that."

And we were back to that again.

Once inside my room, I noticed Ty had on different clothes and the hair near his neck was damp like he had recently showered. Considering he just learned about showers a few days ago, he seemed to be adapting well considering it appeared his world was technology-free.

"My magic's not working, anyway. I don't think I'll be much of a help."

Ty tilted his chin. "What do you mean?"

"You know last night, where I tried to get rid of the magic sight, but it faltered?"

Ty nodded.

"Well, I tried a few more things today—things I knew I could do—and nothing happened. It's like this summer after I tried to use my magic. It was spotty. Sometimes it'd work, and other times, it didn't. It wasn't until I moved here that it became more consistent."

Ty rubbed his chin, then his eyes focused on the little pewter dragon I purchased yesterday perched on my desk. "Let me get rid of this."

"No. Why?"

"It might be laced with an anti-magic spell. It all started when you picked this up yesterday."

He was right. I didn't know what other explanation there was. I nodded, and he took off with my statue.

While he was gone, this was my opportunity to claim the bed. Hmm. I could even lock him out of my room. My smile quickly melted, remembering that he was doing me a favor. I got ready for bed and climbed beneath my blanket.

I was so tired after not sleeping last night, and from all my failed attempts at magic, that I spread my arms out as wide as I could and fell asleep, right in the middle of the bed well before Ty returned.

Chapter 18

When my alarm buzzed the next morning, I shut it off and stretched, enjoying all the room I had. My eyes shot open. Had Ty not returned last night? I rolled over to see him lying on a blanket on the floor with his sleepy eyes only half open and a big smile on his lips.

"Morning, Princess," he said.

I moaned and rolled over, but not before seeing Ty pull himself to his feet and sit beside me in bed. This morning, he only wore a pair of Geoff's sweatpants. His chest was bare, and I was happy he hadn't crawled in bed with me last night. My hands might have had a mind of their own.

"Try your magic now," he encouraged, taking my medallion off my desk and placing it in my hand.

"I am, and you're still here."

He chuckled and gave my shoulder a shake. "Come on. Try something."

I looked over to the flower thriving in the water and focused on the metal in my hand, wishing for one blossom to wilt and die and another to flourish.

Nothing happened.

I scooted to the foot of my bed and focused on the flowers again, taking my time to gather my magic and urge it to the plants.

Still nothing.

I shook my head. "It's gone."

Ty moved down the bed and scooted next to me. His fingers touched the stone on the leather bracelet I wore. "Where did you get that?"

"It doesn't matter."

He grabbed my wrist, twisting the stone in its leather mount. "Then tell me *when* you got it? Did it coincide with your loss of powers?"

"Saturday." My stomach swirled. It did coincide with the troubles I was having.

"From Liam?" Ty asked.

I laughed. "You don't like him, do you?"

Ty dropped my hand. "It's just a bit coincidental, don't you think?"

Was Ty insinuating Liam was blocking my magic? "My magic barely even worked before I met Liam. You're just jealous."

"Jealous?" he laughed and raised an eyebrow. "Of that bumbling fool? If I wanted you, I could have you."

"Really? Cause I'm starting to think you do want me, and you're not getting very close to the prize."

I didn't know what I expected from him, but throwing on the rest of his clothes and heading out the door wasn't it. As he walked down the hallway, he called over his shoulder. "And even if I did want you, it means nothing. I'm going home as soon as possible!"

"Good riddance!" I locked the door behind him, but my heart wasn't behind my words.

I picked up the blanket he had slept on and folded it, threw Geoff's clothes back into the bag, and just like that, all signs of Ty were gone. There was so much more I had to learn from him about my magic...and I wanted to hear about his world. Were there magic schools? What was it like living in a place with other people who wore tunics?

Why hadn't I asked him these questions when he was

here?

Instead, I ogled at his body and focused on myself.

And let him rile me up.

Out of my closet poked Luke's head.

I smiled. He was here just when I needed a friend.

"You can come out. He's gone."

Luke opened his mouth, and the nearly silent little creature let out a tiny whine.

"Really? Now you decide that you like him?"

Luke shook his head.

"Yup, I didn't think so." But I realized something I didn't want to admit.

I was the one who liked him...even if only a little.

Like when he wasn't being a stubborn, arrogant ass. Which wasn't often.

And I wasn't mad at him for anything, I just liked to get a rise out of him...

Like he liked to get from me.

I grabbed my things and headed to the shower. There was no way I was going to be late for class today, but just as I was stepping out of my dorm, my phone rang.

The number was local—at least local to my hometown of Arcola.

"Hello?" I answered.

"Hi, is this Ruby Swanson?"

"Yup."

"It's Margie Smith from Cozy Homes Real Estate. We haven't had much interest in your house, so I was wondering if we could do a price drop and an open house this Sunday."

My stomach clenched. "A price drop? How much?" I already thought the house was priced way lower than it was worth, but the agent had told me the closer we got to winter, the less chance the house would sell this year. I didn't want to think of the bills I'd have to pay to keep it around when nobody lived there.

"Five-thousand."

What was I going to do? I'd spend close to that in heat, electricity, and taxes the longer I kept it. "Whatever you think. You're the expert."

She gave me the details of the open house that she'd run from noon until two o'clock on the upcoming Sunday and that hopefully, it'd bring in an offer. It made my house one of the cheapest four bedrooms in my entire hometown.

When I was done, my stomach was in knots. I tried not to think about selling that house, but the real estate agent's call reminded me how unsettled I still was. After that day with the Salvation Army over a month ago, I didn't clean the house out any further. It was still filled with many of my mom's things, and they belonged with the home. Maybe the next owner would need some furnishings.

The house was a bit of a mess and could use a thorough cleaning. My stomach turned, but I knew I had to head back home to tidy things up before the open house on Sunday.

The morning was moving too fast. I put my phone down and headed to the shower. I didn't have much time if I was going to make sure to make it to class on time. I needed a few minutes with Liam before the professor started his lecture.

***

I flew through the lecture hall doors with eight minutes to spare. I settled down beside Liam with my hand on the bracelet on my wrist. After a bit of small talk about how we enjoyed our study date last night, I worked up the nerve to question him about the gift he had given me.

Not that I believed Ty, but there was something wonky with my magic. Maybe it'd get better now that the dragon statue was gone, but it hadn't yet.

"Hey Liam, I've been meaning to ask you something. I love this bracelet you gave me and thought my friend back in Arcola would like a similar one." It wasn't quite a lie. The thick leather strap and the colorful stone was Sonja's style. She would love it, not that I was planning on getting her one—at least not right now—especially if it was a magic neutralizing item. "I was wondering where you picked it up."

Liam stared at my wrist, then looked up to me with an expressionless face. "I'd rather not say."

"Oh, come on. You'd make her day." Why didn't he want to tell me?

"How about I pick one up for you? That way, you don't find out my secrets, and I'll still make your friend's day." He smiled.

"You don't have to do that for me. I'm happy to take care of it myself."

Now, a slow smile formed on his lips. "It's no bother at all. The bracelet was a gift, and if you found out how much I paid or where it's from, some of that magic goes away."

Magic? Hmm. If he knew what Ty accused the bracelet of being, perhaps he wouldn't have used that term. I took a deep breath. Liam was keeping his mouth shut.

"Wanna study again tonight?" he asked.

My stomach clenched. "I think I'm going to take tonight off." I needed some time to think, plus tonight was reserved for my weekly call to Sonja. I could use an old friend, anyway. Something gold caught my attention at the front of the classroom. Luke hopped up on top of the lecture podium and tapped the microphone which was off. Phew.

Liam looked disappointed.

"How about tomorrow night? I'll have tonight to get caught up, then we'll dig right back into economics."

He nodded as the professor took his place in front of the class, and Luke hopped off his podium, knocking a piece of paper onto the ground. The professor picked it up like nothing had happened, but I snickered.

All through class, I kept rubbing the bracelet I wore. I turned it over and examined how tightly the leather was tied to my wrist. I fiddled with the knots, but Liam looked over and I stopped. That would be a project for later.

If Ty was right, and I still wasn't saying he was, maybe if I took the bracelet off for a while, my magic would return.

Then I would know there was something odd going on. That would mean that Liam either accidentally gave me—the only witch I knew—a bracelet that neutralized magic, or he wasn't what he appeared.

But I had seen him down on Kirkwood Avenue when I had my magic vision, and he didn't appear any different than anyone else. He wasn't magical, that was clear, but I only knew a tiny bit about magic. Maybe there was something I didn't know.

I was paranoid, and it was Ty's fault. Ty was ruining my relationship with Liam. Maybe it was Ty I should be suspecting. He was a dragon hunter. He was a thief, stealing dragon treasure. Maybe I had something he wanted…

Like Luke.

Was my magic somehow protecting my dragon?

I didn't know, but I could ask Luke that question. It was a simple yes or no and he seemed to understand me.

As soon as I settled into my next class—one where Liam wasn't with me, I worked at the bracelet's knots with my fingers. As the professor lectured and the tips of my fingers grew red from manipulating the knot, I realized that the leather was too tight to remove. If I wanted it off, I'd have to cut it— and then Liam would surely know I removed it. How would I explain that?

As I climbed my dorm's stairs, my heart raced from more than the steps. As much as I didn't want to admit it, I hoped Ty was waiting for me. The details of why he stormed out slipped away, and I kept thinking about our day searching for the portal together and the way his presence alleviated my loneliness differently from Liam. When I turned down my hallway and spotted my empty door, my shoulders sagged. It was for the best, I told myself. I tried to remind myself of his stubbornness with not giving up my bed, of how he folded his arms and set his jaw when arguing with me, but for a moment, I found it cute.

My hand twisted my bracelet. I needed it off, no matter what Liam thought. I needed to see if what Ty had said was true. Inside my room, I took a scissors and snipped the knot, causing the leather strap to fall off my wrist. I rubbed my reddened skin from the constant pulling and tugging today. I already felt better.

Now to see if Ty was right. I tucked the bracelet away in my jewelry box and took out my medallion instead.

I looked to a tiny flower on my desk. I dug deep for my magic and channeled it through the silver coin, repeating the magic spell I had tried this morning, wanting one flower to flourish at the expense of the other.

When I opened my eyes, nothing happened. I tried again with the same result.

Perhaps it wasn't the bracelet.

My heart pounded as I pictured Ty, leaning lazily in my bed. He had me doing all sorts of crazy things. Now, I had cut the bracelet off. Was that his plan all along? How would I explain that to Liam?

I grit my teeth and picked up my phone. I needed normal, and thanks to Ty, that wasn't Liam anymore. I dialed Sonja.

"Hey girl!" She was perky. "I was excited about our phone call all day!"

"We don't have to wait a whole week between calls."

"Oh, come on. It adds to the importance of the call, don't you think? I have a whole week of crazy parent stories to tell, and I can't wait to hear about how your night on the town last week went."

My night on the town? That's right. A week ago had been when I ditched Liam and Kat at Young Monsters because I spilled my drink on Ty. I laughed. "A lot has changed since then. I have a new boyfriend."

"You do? Dish. What's his name? Is he hot?"

Hot? "His name's Liam, and he's good looking. Tall and athletic with nice eyes. I don't know. I'm not good at that." All I could think was he didn't have Ty's chiseled physique or his vibrant green stare that went right to my soul. Now, Ty—with his shirt off—was hot. Liam? I'd have to see him undressed, and I'd be able to answer that question.

"Maybe we could meet up this weekend? I could meet

him and tell you how he rates."

It was too early. I didn't want to commit to that yet. Besides, I just took Liam's bracelet off—not completely trusting him yet. Maybe in a few weeks... "I was thinking about coming home this weekend, but I won't be bringing Liam. The Realtor called and wanted to have an open house on Sunday. I thought it would be wise to spiff the place up some."

"Oooh, I'll help. There's no way my parents will say no to me helping you clean. They love you."

I laughed. "Well, now, it's set. I'm coming home this weekend, no matter what. I can't wait to see you!"

"Same here!"

We finished up the call with some chit chat about her boyfriend and some stories about her being the only college student with a curfew, and when I hung up, I was feeling a ton better. I plopped down in bed and pulled out my calculus book, deciding to work on something besides economics. It's not like I needed much calc practice, since math always came easy to me.

Luke appeared on the foot of my bed. I expected him to be distracting, but instead, he cuddled up on my blanket.

"Hey Luke, does my magic protect you? I mean, are you safe with me because of my magic somehow?"

He lifted his head, with heavy eyelids, and shrugged. He then set his head down and fell asleep. So much for Luke's help.

But after about an hour of calc, I followed Luke's lead and fell fast asleep.

Chapter 19

The long-sleeve t-shirt I wore to school the next day succeeded in making Liam not notice that I wasn't wearing his bracelet during economics, but I didn't know how I'd hide it during our study date.

I admit it, guilt drove me to invite Liam to my place to study. I didn't bring him upstairs, a bit of fear—and possibly hope—that Ty would be leaning against my door. We utilized one of the rooms off the lobby, with a big oak table and a little lime green vinyl sofa. I closed the door, keeping the room to ourselves.

Liam pulled his textbook out of his bag and laid it on the table, but I took a seat on the sofa instead. I patted the cushion beside me. As ridiculous as it was, Sonja's question weighed heavily on my mind. Was Liam hot?

I don't know why I hesitated. His toothy grin was sweet. His height, light brown hair, and hazel eyes were just intense enough to make him stand out from a crowd. I looked at the way his t-shirt hugged his chest, seeing defined muscles underneath—but not overwhelming—and I saw no flaws in his appearance. He even dressed nice in dark jeans and polos or vintage style t-shirts. On top of this, he treated me better than any other boyfriend had—with flowers and gifts. Everything about him screamed boyfriend material.

"You took it off." Liam nodded at my wrist.

I glanced down, wrapping my hand around where the bracelet had been to hide the bareness from Liam. While I was checking Liam out, for Sonja's benefit, of course, I forgot to keep my sleeve low. "I did. It was…bothering me." Wasn't a lie. "It was tied too tightly." Yup, still not a lie. The leather *knot* was too tight.

Liam's features hardened, defining the ridges of his cheekbones like I hadn't seen them before. Did he think I didn't appreciate his gift? "I really like your bracelet, I just needed to take it off." He seemed to scoot away, with his focus turning distant.

That's when I realized all the signs I had been giving him. On our date last week to Prego's and the walk along the river, I had stopped kissing him. I pulled away because thoughts of Geoff filled my head. I hadn't seemed eager for our study dates, pushing back the time and days he wanted to meet, and I wouldn't take him up to my place. Now, I cut off his bracelet. He put himself out there, diving head-first into a relationship with me, and all I did was push him away.

If I wasn't careful, I'd lose him. Then when Ty went back to his realm, I'd be here all alone depending on what happened with Luke. I took Liam's hand. "I like you. I really do. I'm working on a new strap for the stone so I can wear it again."

He turned towards me, and my eyes fell upon his lips. I needed to show him I meant my words. I glanced over to confirm the door was closed while scooting closer to Liam, pressing my chest lightly against his bicep and running my hand up his arm. When he didn't pull away, I reached up and turned his head towards me, pressing my lips to his. His kiss was hesitant at first, but when I pressed my body tighter to his, he kissed me back. What started as hesitation turned into eagerness. His tongue met mine as he laid me back on the sofa, placing his body lengthwise along mine. His hand brushed my cheek, and he pulled away enough to say, "Ruby, I really like you, too."

I laughed. This is what we needed to strengthen whatever was between us.

His hand slipped under my shirt, holding my sides, skin against skin. My thoughts I had while on the phone surfaced, wondering how Liam's chest looked compared to Ty's. I slipped my hand under his shirt, feeling his abdomen for the ripples I saw with Ty's.

They were there, much leaner and less pronounced, but I inched his shirt up higher. Liam caught the hint, stopping our kisses to whip the shirt off over his head.

There he was with a bare upper body and something felt a bit off. Maybe it was our location. I should invite him back to my room for somewhere more private, but as he kissed me again, I didn't stop him.

There was no need to run into Ty.

But I stopped his hands as they slipped further up my sides. It's not that I wasn't ready for more, heck, I had done a ton more with Geoff, but…the moment and the place wasn't right. "We should study," I whispered. "And this room isn't exactly secure."

Liam pulled his hands off my torso and sat up. Just like that, he turned it off. "You're probably right. Let's get back to studying. We'll save it for another day."

As Liam slipped his shirt back on and scooted to the table with his notes and a book open in front of him, I wondered how he had halted the passion so quickly. I, on the other hand, needed a few minutes. Heck, I'd probably have my mind in the gutter all night with thoughts of Liam—and, I hated to admit it, but Ty.

We reviewed pages of notes, and the next chapter of the

text, but then the door creaked open.

"Oh, sorry. I didn't realize anyone was in here. We had this room reserved for seven PM." Three girls stood outside the door, each holding a pile of books.

I looked down to my phone. "No problem. It was open, so we took advantage of the private space. We're pretty much done."

I stood up and threw my things into my bag, my eyes darting to the couch Liam and I had been on less than an hour earlier.

"Liam, I'm going to head upstairs. I need..." a cold shower "...to go over some calculus notes before bed. I'll catch ya tomorrow?"

His eyebrows wrinkled together, but when I stepped up on my tippy toes and gave him a kiss, he nodded. "Sounds good. See you in the morning."

We headed out the door and each went our own direction. Liam out the front entrance of my dorm, and me up the stairs with thoughts of the date in my head. It had been so long since I was in such a new relationship that I forgot how awkward it was. For some reason, we didn't say exactly what we were thinking. We were still getting used to how each other's bodies felt and things were...well...different.

Maybe it was because I spent so many years with Geoff...and he was the only other boyfriend I had. Would I compare everyone to him for the rest of my life?

That's when I realized when I was kissing Liam, it wasn't Geoff I was comparing him to.

It was Ty. GASP!

As I exited on the seventh floor and turned the corner to head down my hall, there was the man I was thinking about. Ty leaned against my door with dripping wet hair and wearing nothing but a towel around his waist. Way to be inconspicuous in this girls-only dorm.

He pushed his hair out of his eyes and smiled when he saw me.

And I couldn't help it. My heart pitter-pattered. Call it pent-up emotions from my study date, but I couldn't take my eyes off him.

Now, Ty, was hot.

Smokin' hot.

"Come back for some clean clothes?" I tried my best to keep my emotions inconspicuous. Ty didn't need to know I was happy he was back, but I tried too hard and my words were a bit harsh. "Well, you can't have them."

Ty didn't seem to mind my tone. He shook his head and shifted his weight so I could unlock my door. He leaned close, his warm, fresh breath upon my neck. "I'm not back for my clothes." He brushed my hair off my shoulder and brought his mouth closer to my skin. "I came back for you."

Chapter 20

I stiffened and stepped away from my dorm, leaving my key in the lock. "You came back for me?" I laughed. "What do you mean?" Ty needed me to find the portal, that I knew, but my magic was gone. I knew what a man in a towel outside my door insinuated, but I didn't want to jump to any conclusions—even though my insides happily made those assumptions.

How could I just have been making out with Liam and now, Ty caused my hormones to flare?

Ty finished unlocking my door for me and stepped inside my room. "Come on, nobody saw me yet. You don't want to change that, do you?"

I shook my head, staring at the ripples on Ty's abdomen as he squatted beside the plastic bag filled with Geoff's clothing. The towel split, showing off a muscular thigh. He pulled out a pair of athletic pants and slipped them on under his towel, letting the towel fall to the ground. Geoff's pants hung low on Ty, and my eyes settled at the waistband. That's when it hit me. While I was kissing Liam, the sensation that it was wrong and I should stop wasn't because of Liam, our location, or that I wasn't over Geoff.

It was because I wanted Ty.

And it wasn't purely for his body…nor his boyish charm.

When I was with Ty, I felt taken care of. Comfortable. He gave me all his attention and made me feel special, like Mom used to make me feel.

I forced my eyes up to the dimple on his chin and

reminded myself that Ty would be leaving me as soon as I found his portal. "How long were you waiting for me?"

"Not long. I saw you and Liam downstairs." Ty glanced at my bare wrist where my sleeve was pushed up revealing the lack of Liam's bracelet. He then looked into my eyes with a softness that made me forget whatever it was that Ty had done to make me mad…and made me want to kiss him. I licked my lips, and a flash of desire that had to match my own sparkled in Ty's eyes, but he quickly looked away. Had I been too harsh on him before? Was I the one that was a pain in the butt?

"I'm sorry—" We both said the words in unison.

My heart pounded standing so close to him. I went left to get some space between us, but Ty must have had the same plan and we ended up bumping into each other.

Ty glanced up and that desire I saw before intensified, causing my entire body to warm. I needed to get a grip on my excitement tonight before…

I couldn't finish my thought. Ty nearly dived forward as his mouth hungrily found mine. I stiffened and lifted my hands to push him away, but when they fell on his bare chest, I relaxed into him instead as he wrapped his strong arms around me.

His kiss was moist, yet hard against my lips like we were joined together as close as possible from a single kiss. His tongue swiped between my teeth, and I eagerly met him, sliding my hands off his chest and wrapping them around his solid torso. I wanted more, but it appeared, Ty didn't. He pulled away, giving me a view of his back for the first time and my heart dropped at the scars upon it. One long line of claw marks was fresh, swollen, yet scabbed over. Ty chose to live a hard life.

His hand rubbed the back of his neck as he dropped down onto my bed. "That's not good for either of us."

My fingers rubbed my lips, the memory of him still there. I wouldn't argue, and Ty voiced what had been going through my head.

"I'm going back home as soon as I can. This isn't a place I can stay."

And as I looked at the scarred dragon tattoo on his chest, I knew that was true.

"So, why did you come back to my dorm then?" My words were harsher than I wanted, but my emotions were raw and on the surface.

He shrugged. "Because I told you that I could have you if I wanted."

My jaw dropped, and I tensed.

Ty's eyes jetted back and forth, following the contours of my face, then he stood up, taking me into his arms, but I pushed him away. "Ruby, that was just a joke. I didn't mean to offend you again."

"You do that a lot because you're not funny. You're just an ass."

He chuckled. "Well then, that'll make our working relationship much easier." He lifted his necklace over his head and held it out to me. "I thought this might be able to help us find the portal."

I crossed my arms and didn't take the necklace. "I don't think I want to help you anymore. I completed my end of the deal, spending an entire day looking for your portal and giving you a place to stay. You're on your own, now."

Ty nodded at the necklace, unaffected by my words. "Don't you want to know what it is?"

"Not really." I shrugged. Maybe that was a lie. The necklace had glowed when I had my magic vision.

Ty hopped up on my bed and slid back. "My mother gave it to me when I was young. I've worn it every day." Ty ran his fingers along the worst of his scars that were over his heart. "It's what kept me alive."

"If you didn't steal from dragons, you wouldn't have that trouble."

Ty shook his head. "This scar wasn't from a dragon. It was from a witch."

I sat down at my desk, all memories of our kiss, and my anger gone. "How did a witch do that?"

"It was nothing more than revenge. My parents discovered the witch was practicing black magic, and the witch tried to hide by casting a spell on them that rotted out their hearts and their family's hearts. My parents and siblings died. The poison ate at my skin." Ty circled the scar with his finger, seeming to gather his thoughts. "But many years before that, my mother had given me this charm. It was blessed by another witch with a protection spell. As soon as my poisoned skin touched this charm, the blackness receded, and I healed—well, at least I healed physically, but then I was twelve and had lost my family. The poison had wiped out everyone I had loved." Ty leaned back in bed and stared at the ceiling, laying the charm on his bare chest. "It's kept me alive for ten years since then."

I couldn't help myself. I got out of my chair and crossed my room, sitting beside Ty in my bed. I lifted the charm from off his chest. "And how do you think this will help me?"

He sat up and helped drape the necklace over my head.

"Here, in this world, I don't seem to need it. There are no dragons or witches after me. Now you, maybe it'll protect you from whatever is blocking your magic."

I wrapped my hand around the stone, feeling small zaps of electricity. I let it drop against my shirt. "How do you stand that?"

"Stand what?"

"The pain when it touches your skin."

Ty tilted his chin and touched the jade circle. "I don't feel anything. It must be because you're a witch."

Ty was extremely close to me, and I could smell a combination of soap and a warm fall day coming from his skin. He looked up, focusing on my lips and just when I thought he'd kiss me again, he leaned back and smiled.

"Come on. Try your magic again."

I nodded, turning towards the two flowers on my desk. Before my eyes, one grew roots and the other wilted.

I didn't even have to focus.

Ty hooted a cheer. "That's how easy it should be!"

I turned towards him. Was it really that easy? I tried something else, and in a moment, Ty and I had swapped places.

"Whoa," Ty said, holding his head. "That wasn't expected."

"My magic's working." It was true. Magic was as easy as talking. As easy as walking. My magic was a part of me.

"Not the magic, but what you just did. I've never seen anyone swap places before. It must be your special skill."

"What do you mean?"

"Each witch has something specific they can do that all others cannot. Some can fertilize fields and make plants grow, others can cause illness." Ty ground his teeth together. There was more to that story.

"Is there somewhere in your world I can go to learn more about magic?" I couldn't believe I even asked that question. "A school, perhaps?" Not that I could get away from my life here. I had too many ties to college and to the house I owned, but the thought of following Ty home gave me a bit of excitement.

"No magic schools. Parents teach children magic."

And my parent had abandoned me. I pulled Ty's necklace off. "I can't take this from you."

"Oh, come on. I'll want it back when we find the portal, of course, but until then, it's yours."

I smiled shyly, then leaned forward and placed a small kiss on Ty's cheek. "Thank you."

He turned towards me, lifted his hand and rubbed his thumb under my eye. He didn't say anything, but he didn't have to. For some strange reason, I believed he'd do whatever he could to keep me safe.

Chapter 21

After a few hours of magic practice that made me completely exhausted, I crashed on my bed with Ty beside me. I curled towards the wall, and he laid on his back with his warm side pressed against my body.

"Tell me about your world," I said between a yawn.

Ty's voice was soft and relaxing as he told me about kingdoms and castles. Dragons, witches, and what it was like without any technology at all.

"I'm surprised you do so well here," I said, turning over to face him. "You don't seem overwhelmed with cars, phones, computers, or even a simple light switch."

He looked at me with lazy, proud eyes. "I'm very adaptable."

I laughed. "I see that."

"Have you been here before?"

Ty shook his head. "No, but there are stories that are told to children of this world. Many stories that most think are fiction. The stories tell of your airplanes, cars, and even your flushing toilets. Don't you have stories of my world, too?"

My hand had a mind of their own as it placed itself on Ty's side, feeling the hardness beneath the simple black t-shirt he had gotten out of the bag from Geoff. "Yes, we have stories, TV shows, and movies of your world, or worlds similar to yours."

"So, if you came to my world, would you be overwhelmed by kings and queens, castles, magical creatures, or horse and buggies?"

"Depends how much trouble they caused me!"

Ty placed his rough hand on top of mine, holding my palm flat against his stomach. "I think you'd be just fine." He smiled.

I shook my head. "I don't know if I could survive without showers, microwaves, or mochas. Tell me more of your world."

"Very well." Ty's words were like a bedtime story as he went on and on about kingdom politics, games children played, and the foods he missed. His voice lulled me into the deepest sleep I had had in a long time. It felt like he was my best friend and we had no secrets between us.

My alarm went off the next morning, and I found Ty's arm draped across my chest. His face nuzzled in my neck, and we fit together—when we weren't at each other's throat.

I had learned over the past few days to give myself lots of time for school so I wasn't late, and I had half an hour yet before I had to be out of bed.

Ty's eyes opened, but he squinted at the light.

"Good morning," I whispered.

A slow smile grew on his lips when I snuggled closer to him. We might not want to start any type of relationship, but for a minute or two, I'd take the comfort Ty offered. It appeared he relished in the companionship I offered, too. After hearing about the death of his parents last night, it seemed like we shared a silent connection that I didn't have with anyone else. Not Sonja and not even Luke.

"How exactly did you get here?" I asked. "Did this portal suck you through, or something else?"

"I followed a gem dragon."

I tensed a bit beside him as I thought more about Luke. "Tell me about the gem dragons."

"They come in all sorts of colors and sizes, but like I said, they're much smaller than the other dragons. The one I followed was a light shade of gold with red, glowing eyes."

I scooted away from Ty. I had known he was here hunting Luke, but I didn't want to admit it. Was this soft side of Ty all an act? Did he know Luke was connected to me? The first time I bumped into Ty, it was outside the lecture hall at school where Luke was causing mischief during class. Was Ty only getting closer to me to find Luke? Maybe I had been wrong that there were no secrets between us. "Are you still after the dragon?" I tensed and pulled away, but Ty's arm was strong and kept me near.

Ty laughed and shook his head. "There's no treasure here for me. I hunted the wrong dragon. The rest of his pride used him as a decoy, but I didn't realize that until it was too late."

So, that's how Luke suddenly ended up back in my world. He had used the portal. Maybe my dragon would know how to get Ty home, and I wouldn't need magic at all. My heart beat quickly. Should I tell Ty about Luke? It was the only secret I was keeping. Maybe if he promised to not hunt him. He did already say that he wasn't after Luke anymore… Oh, I was so conflicted. How much did I trust this man lying beside me in bed?

Enough to let him sleep in the same room with me. In the same bed with his arms around me. Even if Ty frustrated me at times, he had never lied to me—not that I was aware of.

But trust a dragon hunter with the location of a dragon? I needed to talk to Luke first.

I crawled over Ty to get out of bed, and I wouldn't deny I liked doing it. In fact, I may have moved extra slow as a bit of a tease. As I gathered my things for the shower, I looked back to him lying lazily in my bed. "Portal hunting tonight?"

He smiled. "I can't wait."

And honestly, neither could I.

* * *

As I slipped into my seat beside Liam, my thoughts were on Ty. So much so, I didn't see Geoff follow me down and sit behind me in Kat's old seat.

"Are you free tonight?" Geoff whispered, causing me to jump.

"No, I have plans." Argh! Why did I say that? Geoff through me off-guard.

"Shouldn't you be sitting by your girlfriend?" I couldn't help my evil tongue.

Geoff shook his head. "Elaina isn't my girlfriend."

"Could have fooled me. Did you break up already?"

Geoff tightened his lips like he did when I guessed something right. Adult life was hard, wasn't it? "How about I come over and get my things tonight? We should talk."

"You can't," I snapped, a bit too sharp. "I already gave them away, plus, we have nothing to talk about. There is nothing between us anymore." I was surprised at the conviction in my words. Two weeks later, and I was already over Geoff. Perhaps I never knew what true love was. "And, why are you interested in me now? After waiting an entire year to break up with me, now, you want to spend time with me again?"

Geoff's jaw fell open and his eyebrows narrowed. "I—I didn't want to break up with you for an entire year."

"But you told me that when you dumped me."

Geoff shook his head, causing his brown bangs to fall over an eye. "That's not what I meant. Sure, I had been thinking about it off an on for a while, but we had a lot of good times. I was hoping my confusion would pass."

"Well, you should have told me. We should have talked about it before I moved here to be with you."

Geoff tightened his lips, and he looked like he was going to argue, but Liam came to the rescue and I appreciated it. I didn't want to argue with Geoff. I just wanted him out of my life.

Liam hung his hand over the back of his seat. "I don't think we've actually met. I'm Liam, Ruby's boyfriend."

I cringed, but there it was. Liam was my boyfriend, and I had cheated on him by kissing Ty. It's not like we had the whole exclusive dating conversation yet...but it was wrong. All I could think about was Ty and because of that, I knew that Liam might think he was my boyfriend, but I knew he wasn't—he really had never been. Everything was right about Liam; except he was wrong for me. I had to put an end to this, but now wasn't the time while the professor began his lecture.

Liam leaned over and whispered his request again, "Study date tonight?"

I shook my head. "I can't. And I've got to go back home this weekend and take care of my house."

"Your house?" He arched an eyebrow.

"Long story, but yup, I have a house. We'll have to chat on Monday. Maybe I'll be back here Sunday afternoon." And hopefully, I knew what the heck I was doing by then. Maybe Ty would be gone after tonight, and then I could focus on my life here...you know, in this non-magical world.

The professor cleared his throat, and we dropped the

conversation.

* * *

Ty wasn't waiting outside my dorm that afternoon, and my chest hollowed as I fumbled with my lock. We left on good terms, so he should be here—unless he found the portal on his own. Would he leave without saying goodbye?

As I pushed the door open, I smiled to see Ty on my bed. He set a book aside and hopped to his feet, leaving the messenger bag he was never without in his place.

"What are you doing?" I asked, nodding towards the worn book laying on top of my comforter.

"I picked it up down in the lobby this morning. I didn't go anywhere today. The story sucked me in."

I peered over him to read the title: *The Princess Bride*. I laughed. "Not what I expected you to read."

"Have you read it?"

I shook my head. "I've seen the movie like a dozen times."

"Does that mean you know what's in this book?"

That's when I stopped. As much as Ty told me last night, there still was so much in my world he didn't know anything about, yet he seemed to get along just fine. He was smart and adaptable…and could read, apparently.

"Well, the book is hilarious," Ty said. "A fire swamp? Really? Pit of despair? Who thinks this stuff up?"

"And dragons and black magic curses from witches? If your world exists, maybe the world of Princess Buttercup and Westley exists, too."

Ty laughed. "I hope so. Wouldn't it be fun to visit?

Maybe when we find the portal…"

That's when I remembered that I was looking for Luke. If Luke would just take us there, this could be over.

When Ty tucked the book on my desk and sat across from me, giving my legs an excited pat, I knew I didn't want this to end, but I promised him I'd help him back home. I knew how important home was to a person, and I wouldn't deprive him of that.

"Okay. Ready? Magic sight, here we come. You'll be my ears, again?" Butterflies danced in my stomach. A whole evening of holding Ty's hand sounded like an adventure I didn't want to miss.

I pulled my medallion from my pocket and wrapped my hand around the stone of Ty's necklace, pulling in the vision to see magic in exchange for my sense of taste and hearing. The magic was slower than I experienced with Ty last night, but it came. When I opened my eyes, my body glowed. Ty smiled and moved his lips, but I shook my head. "I can't hear you."

He nodded. I looked around my room, and my eyes locked onto something inside my open jewelry box that was glowing. I set the medallion I held down on the desk, and reached into my little wooden box, pulling out a glowing gem attached to a leather wristband.

My heart stopped.

The bracelet from Liam had been magical. It probably was what was responsible for my faulty magic.

But why?

I pulled the bracelet out and laid it on my desk beside the coin. It definitely was magic. I looked up to Ty, and he seemed to understand what I was thinking. I gripped my medallion and wished the magic sight away and the return of my other senses. I needed to take care of this before I found Ty's portal and was forced to say goodbye.

Chapter 22

"You were right! Liam was trying to stop me from using magic. Why? Why would he do that? Why would it matter to him?" I paced what little floor space I had in my tiny dorm, glancing at the bracelet on my desk.

Ty sat on the edge of my bed with his hands folded in his lap, appearing so much less menacing than he truly was. "People block magic all the time."

"Not in my world, Ty. Not here."

He shrugged. "I've seen magic blocked to keep someone under control or because they wanted to steal something that was being protected by magic."

"I have nothing. Until meeting you, I didn't even know how to use my magic. Heck, I still really don't! Come on. Let's go." I waved him towards the door.

"Where are we going?"

"To find and confront Liam. He lives down on Kirkwood above that antique store. Let's hope he's home."

Ty scrambled to his feet, and he stood between me and the door. "Ruby, that's not wise. What if he's a witch himself? What if he has something in store for you that we don't know?"

"He's not a witch. He didn't glow with my magic vision."

"Remember what I said about blocking magic? Maybe he's hiding who he really is."

I shrugged, holding Ty's necklace in my hand. "Well, I have this. If it's as powerful as you say it is, I'm safe. He's the one that should worry."

Ty leaned back on my door. "I can't let you leave. Not

until we figure out what we're up against."

I scooped the bracelet off my desk. "I need answers, and I need them now." I pulled at my magic, intending to swap places with Ty, putting him in my spot and me by the door, but nothing happened. I tried again, but nothing. I tossed the bracelet down on my desk. "Now, I can't even touch that thing!"

"Hey, Ruby. Calm down. Be smart about this situation. You might only get one chance to figure out what's going on." He picked up the bracelet and turned it over in his hand, then tucked it away in my jewelry box again. "It could be nothing. Maybe he just stumbled upon the stone like you did that dragon in the antique store. Or maybe, someone else gave it to him and is behind everything. We don't know the details."

I willed my heart to calm, but it didn't.

"You could ruin your relationship with him over something he's oblivious to."

My heart rate only picked up. "Ruin my relationship with him? Ha! That's been ruined since the moment you took your shirt off in front of me and escorted me on the most adventurous, fun date I ever had looking for a dumb portal."

Ty chuckled. "There, there. Feeling better?"

Not quite. "And then you come into my room and lay on my bed. You stand outside my door wearing nothing but a towel. Then, you kiss me like I've never been kissed before! Do you think that there's any hope of having a relationship with anyone else but you?"

Ty stopped chuckling. His boyish face turned serious, and I finally saw his twenty-two years in his eyes. He slowly walked up to me and placed his hand on my cheek.

This time, his kiss was soft, hesitant even. He sucked

on my bottom lip and let go, only to repeat the gesture with my top lip. He leaned against me until my back was flat against the door. I reached for the hem of his shirt and pulled it over his head, and he, in return, did the same with mine. I leaned against his chest with my black, lace bra against his skin, wishing it was off, but knowing that decision wouldn't be wise. It would lead to so much more, and I couldn't get that attached to Ty. In my entire life, all the people I was closest to left me. My dad. My mom. Geoff. And I knew Ty would be next.

"Ruby," Ty breathed into my neck as he placed a kiss against my tender skin. "You've ruined me as well. You're the only woman I've ever known who I could call my equal. You give me crap when I give it to you. You smile and laugh like none other, and you have such a soft heart. Worthy of an entire kingdom."

I drank him in. His warm skin against mine. His lips. His chest, his hips that pressed against my stomach, and I forgot all about Liam. About Geoff. About any other man except for Ty.

But it only lasted a moment before my thoughts returned.

Ty wanted to go home. Needed to go home, and as much as his world intrigued me, it wasn't my home. I regained my focus and stopped kissing him, pulling my head back far enough to whisper. "Okay. I'm ready to find the portal now."

Ty moaned, kissing me again. "Promise me we'll do this one more time before I leave." His lips brushed along my jawline, and my knees weakened.

"I hope more than once." I leaned into Ty's arms and had the magic sight return at the expense of my other senses. "I'm ready," I said. I gave the bracelet on my desk one more glance before I forced myself to head out of the dorm before I did something I couldn't take back.

* * *

We spent all night, walking around town. Down by the waterfall, along the train tracks, and through campus. When I closed my eyes and felt for the warmth of magic, it took us to Kirkwood Avenue again, but we didn't find anything special, nor did we run into Liam. By ten o'clock, we were exhausted and laying side-by-side in bed again. Once I was snuggled in beside Ty, he leaned over, kissed my forehead and said, "Night."

That was it? I wanted more, and I knew he did too, but it wasn't in our cards right now. Neither of us needed the heartbreak. We both had enough of that in our lives already.

When my alarm went off the next morning, a sense of dread filled my chest. I'd need to see Liam in my first class. There was no way I could face him and not say something I might regret. "Come with me," I whispered to Ty who was just waking up. "The classes are so big that you could come along and nobody would know that you weren't a student."

"I think you can handle it. You've calmed down since last night. Just remember to go about it like we practiced."

Once I had my hearing back last night, we spent the evening bouncing all sorts of ideas off each other. The best we came up with was faking an allergic reaction. I knew it was sneaky, but it'd at least get him to tell me where he got the bracelet. I wanted to use my magic to force the truth from his lips, but Ty reminded me that making people do something against their will wasn't possible. We settled for just a little good-old-fashioned trickery.

As I entered the lecture hall, my stomach did flips. It was showtime. Either Liam was the nice boy I had been dating, or he was an evil witch. Unfortunately, after how I'd kissed Ty last night, neither of them were compatible with me…at least not while Ty was in my world.

Liam turned around and smiled as I walked towards him. It was hard to believe that he could be purposefully blocking my magic. What did he want? As I sat down beside him, I didn't pull my desk out. I didn't think I'd be staying here. Up in front of the class, Luke paced. Could he sense my trepidation?

With a fake smile, I greeted Liam. "Good morning!" I pulled the bracelet out of my pocket and flashed it at him. "I'm having a problem with this. It gave me a rash, and I need to know what it's made of or what chemicals are on it. Where did you get it from?"

I held out my wrist to where I had taped a piece of nickel last night. Nickel had always given me a rash, and I was happy to see the blotchy skin this morning. Liam turned my wrist over and ran a finger along my flesh. "I'm sorry, but I can't tell you where it's from because I didn't get it at a store. It was one of the many stones my mom had."

"It's your mom's?"

Liam nodded. "Was my mom's. She died a few years ago."

My heart went out to him, but then, the story was too similar to mine. Was he playing me? He had told me his parents were out of the picture, but I hadn't known that they were dead.

That's when Luke jumped over the seat and landed in

my lap. I jumped back with a start. Liam's eyes widened for a moment, and I studied his face as he seemed to be looking everywhere except where Luke sat.

Could Liam see Luke?

"Well, if you don't want the bracelet, I'll take it back." Liam held out his hand.

"No, it's not that I don't want it. I just can't wear it."

"Here. Hand it over, and I'll get you something else."

I was hesitant, but reached out to give it to Liam. Just as I was about to drop it in his palm, Luke flew up and knocked it out of my hand with his head. When it dropped to the floor, he stood on top of the stone in the center of the leather strap. My dragon shook his head at me.

I snatched it out from under Luke's feet and tucked it into my jean's pocket before Liam even bent over. "The lecture's starting, we'll talk about this later."

Liam scowled as he turned his attention forward. I knew Ty was waiting for me in the commons area, and I couldn't sit through the lecture. I slipped my notebook into my bag, gave Liam a little nod goodbye, and took off out of the room wishing I knew what Liam was after.

I heard Liam behind me, but I didn't want to talk. I plowed through the commons with Luke bouncing beside me, until Ty came into focus. That's when Luke poofed into nothingness. Ty knitted his eyebrows together. I was certain he had seen Luke.

What did that mean?

I didn't wait to find out. I grabbed Ty's arm and dragged him out of the building with a glance over my shoulder to ensure Liam wasn't following me. "I'm going home."

Ty turned down the street my dorm was on, but I pulled him a different way. "Not to my dorm, but to my house. We're going out of town this weekend." I marched down the main street and pulled off into the lot where I stored my car. I knew the two-hundred dollars a month would come in handy. I fumbled through my keys for my key fob, finally unlocking my car doors. "Get in."

Ty hesitated. I supposed he had never ridden in a car, but that only stopped him for a moment. In minutes, we were driving down the main highway, on our way out of this city.

And it felt good. It felt like I was going back to where I belonged.

Chapter 23

As I drove down the highway, Ty didn't say much. He had fumbled to get his seatbelt on, and one hand clenched the door handle while the other braced himself against the console. I was glad he was quiet while what had just happened back at school ran through my head.

Was Liam hiding something?

Was he intentionally blocking my magic, or was it just a stone from his mother—something he knew nothing about? I mean, I did pick up a magic object down at the antique store. They were around, scattered in this world. But Liam and I hadn't been dating that long and if his story was true, that the stone had been his mother's, wasn't it too soon in our relationship to hand such a sentimental object over? I knew I consistently struggled to part with my mom's things.

I had been alone with Liam more than once. He never tried to hurt me. He had been nothing but sweet.

I sucked in my bottom lip. That's what I was afraid of. Leave it to me to sabotage my new relationship. And even worse, I couldn't control myself around Ty. It was almost like—like I purposely picked the man who was the least available, or at least, the least available long-term.

Ty let go of the door handle and began to futz with the seatbelt strap across his chest as we zipped seventy-miles an hour down the highway.

He tucked his hair behind his ears and looked at me with uncertain eyes. "How far away do you live?"

I shrugged. "About two hours. Don't worry. Millions of people ride in cars every day."

Ty looked forward and nodded. The worry lines around his eyes were not easing up, though. Maybe if I distracted him, he'd settle down. We did have a few hours together in the car. He had been so relaxed and adaptable that this was a bit out of character. I guessed everyone had something that made them uncomfortable. I filled in Ty about Liam's odd behavior when I questioned him about the bracelet, and his pushiness to get it back.

"It could be nothing. He could just be upset with you. Upset such a beautiful, intelligent girl is slipping through his fingers." Ty's compliment made my heart flutter, but when I glanced at him, all I saw was his normally tan skin turned as white as a ghost.

"You're carsick. Pull the lever on the side of your seat and lay back. Close your eyes. You'll feel better."

I expected him to be macho and stubborn, but he listened, rummaging with the side of the seat and laying back. He closed his eyes.

Just when I wondered if he had fallen asleep, he spoke, his voice low and weak. "You told me about your dad, but what about your mom? Does she still live where we're going? Siblings?"

My mouth went dry. Ty really didn't know much about me, but I told him the story, trying to get his mind off the drive. "My mom died earlier this year. I don't have any siblings."

"So, you don't have anyone, either."

I swallowed a lump, then I reached over and gave his knee a playful shove. "Not true." He looked over to me, and I smiled. "I have you."

I didn't mean anything by that statement, just a bit of a

tease to make him feel better. I expected him to say something about only until we found the portal, but he didn't. He simply looked back up at the ceiling and closed his eyes again with a small smile.

"Tell me about your family," I said.

His lips pushed together. "There's nothing much to tell. We were close, but then they died. Case closed."

"You had siblings."

Ty turned towards the door, and his voice went low. "I don't want to talk about it right now."

I swallowed. Real bright, Ruby. I had known his entire family was killed by the curse he told me about, and I knew how painful it was to relive memories. I tightened my lips and turned the radio up to keep myself quiet. How had I been so attracted to Ty when we knew nothing about each other and some conversations were so difficult? I slowly rubbed my fingers against my leather steering wheel, wondering what it would be like to lose everyone you loved all at once. Losing my mom had almost killed me. Now, if I would have lost a father and siblings that I was close to as well?

I don't think I'd be strong enough to pull through.

Keeping silent was the easy thing to do. Focusing on the radio, even easier. Avoiding what I was going to say, the best advice.

But I never took good advice.

I clicked the radio off. "My mom was my best friend. We did everything together, since it was only her and me. I told her everything about my life, even..." I cleared my throat. "Even the details about my relationship with Geoff. I never thought I'd lose her." Ty didn't move, so I continued. "It was hard, listening to everyone tell me they were sorry for what happened and how they wished it wouldn't have. Their words were useless to me. I was numb. Everyone said time would heal my wounds, but after five months, they haven't closed yet. In fact, I feel like they're festering and opening. They won't close until...well, I don't know if they ever will."

Slowly, Ty turned back towards me, his face stoic and unchanging while he examined my own solemn expression. Just when I thought I had him feeling better, he turned back to the window. So much for opening up. I reached for the radio, but lowered my hand when Ty placed his upon my thigh. I dropped my hand and took his callused one in mine.

I changed the subject. "So, my mother owned a house. An old Victorian one with three floors and four bedrooms. It costs a fortune to heat, so I'm trying to sell it. My real estate agent is holding an open house this weekend, looking for buyers, and I thought I'd go home to clean it up some. My friend, Sonja, said she'd help, and I need to call her when I'm almost home."

Ty squeezed my hand. "See, you have friends. How can you not? You're like a ray of sunshine."

I laughed. "You're being ridiculous."

He just shook his head and smiled softly, then closed his eyes again. His expression was so conflicting from the playful Ty I knew. Less than an hour ago, his eyes were wide and focused as I came rushing down the hallway at school with Luke skipping beside me.

I even swore his eyes widened when he saw Luke and flashed with a bit of fire...

That was it. Ty might be a dragon hunter, he might even be after Luke, but I had to ask.

My hand tightened on the wheel, and I focused out the

window ahead of me as trees and billboards whipped by. I cleared my throat. "Um…back at school, did you see..." Just spit it out, Ruby. "Did you see a dragon beside me?" I glanced over, to read Ty's expression, but his mouth was open slightly, and I could hear his breathing grow more relaxed. I had seen that look before—he was sleeping.

I turned the radio back on, keeping the volume low. We'd be home in a little over an hour, and I needed the time to think, anyway.

Chapter 24

Butterflies formed in my stomach when the familiar buildings of downtown Arcola passed by my window. I was almost home. Ty stirred beside me, pulling on the lever and sitting up in his seat.

"Feeling better?"

He smiled. "I prefer this speed to dragon highway speed."

I laughed. "Honestly, so do I."

As we drove down my street, I pointed out the front window toward my giant home with the old light blue wood siding in need of a new coat of paint. "That's it. The one with the white shutters and the square corner tower."

"It's nice. Why'd you move away?"

"It's a part of being an adult in this world. You graduate from high school and go away to college."

I parked in the driveway, on top of a huge crack that seemed to be bigger than last time. I cut the engine and flipped through my keys, finding the one for the front door. Swinging my backpack over my shoulder, I took a deep breath. Ty followed me up onto the front porch where the white swing moved slightly in the fall breeze. Memories filled my head of sitting there in the evening with Mom, and I averted my eyes.

The sofa I couldn't part with over a month ago still sat in the center of my living room and the piano was still under the window, but the house was emptier than I remembered. Nothing more was gone, but the lack of my mom's personality here was unsettling. My head was filled with warm memories of my childhood. "Do you mind waiting for your tour? The whole drive here, something's been nagging on me that I need to look up."

Ty nodded and settled onto my sofa. I pulled my laptop from my bag and pushed his legs out of my way to sit beside him. I logged into my neighbor's wi-fi, which they offered to me to save on bills sometime after mom died. I typed in Liam Pennington into Google. Liam had told me the bracelet was his mother's, and that she was dead. Something inside wanted to confirm—or deny—that story.

I couldn't move on. I was hung up on it. I really hoped he was nothing more than a nice college junior who helped a freshman who needed a friend.

Ty sat up and scooted beside me. "What are you looking at?"

"I'm trying to confirm what Liam said." In the search results, Liam's name didn't appear—not at all. "Strange. He's not here."

"Does everyone show up there?" Ty asked. He squinted at the screen. He had seen me use a computer before and he was learning about them quickly. A world without technology was something I hoped I never had to get to know.

I shrugged. "A few mentions, maybe. Here…" I typed my own name into the field and had a few honor roll lists, piano recital brochures, a newspaper article about last year's graduating class, and my mom's obituary show up all on the first page. I ran my finger down the screen, pointing out each time Ruby Campbell was mentioned. "Now, look at this." I typed in Liam Pennington again. Random results of a Liam or a Pennington, but nothing that seemed to match the guy I had been dating.

"What about me?" Ty asked.

"You wouldn't be in here. You're not from here..." My jaw fell open.

"Exactly," Ty said.

Had Liam been from the same place as Ty? I rubbed my temple. He couldn't be. He was enrolled in school like me. Said he was a junior and had been going there for a while already...

But, nobody on campus treated him like they knew him. Maybe I just hadn't run into any of his friends yet. He said he had roommates...

It's like Ty knew what I was thinking. "You asked me to go to class with you this morning. Said anyone could attend because the lecture halls were so large."

I sucked in my bottom lip, logging into my school email, searching through the directory. I typed for his name, but it didn't come up, confirming what I thought.

"Liam isn't enrolled at Bloomington University." My heart sank. What did this all mean?

Ty answered my unasked question. "Ruby, it wasn't an accident that Liam gave you that bracelet. He's after something. Whether he's from this world or mine, it doesn't matter. You need to stay away from him."

I laughed. That was easier said than done.

But it really wasn't that hard. I just needed to call school and alert them about Liam.

But then what would he do? I had already tipped him off that I was suspicious of him and it appeared, he knew a thing or two about magic.

My heart was thumping as my doorbell rang. I jumped, but Ty stood in front of me. I had magic. I could get out of anything, right?

I swallowed. I didn't even know the extent of my magic nor its limitations.

Ty headed towards the entryway, peering around a corner to see out one of the house's many windows. "It's a little blond girl with freckles."

"Little blond girl?" I laughed. He meant it was Sonja. She was quite petite.

I pushed Ty aside and flung open the door, happy to see my friend and get a sense of comfort and safety.

Sonja's laugh was musical as I squeezed her in my arms. "Whoa, girl. Miss me?"

"More than you know!"

Her eyes fluttered behind me, and she clapped. "Goodie. I get to meet your new boyfriend. I thought you weren't ready to bring him home." Before I could stop her, she reached for Ty's hand. "Liam, right?"

"Ty." He glared at me.

I shrugged. "It's been a long few days."

"So, this is someone else? I guess I should have known. You didn't know if Liam was hot, but this guy, he's on fire!"

My chest swelled. Okay, I didn't need Sonja's approval, but man, it felt nice. I felt better in an instant. The good news was I was home, and I didn't have to worry about what to do with Liam until the weekend was over.

"You ready for some massive cleaning?" Sonja walked through my living room and ran a hand down the piano, leaving a streak of clean in her wake. "We're going to sell this house of yours."

I laughed. "I wish I was as eager about it as you."

Sonja draped her arms around my shoulders. "Well, if you don't want to sell it, I'll live here. It'd get me away from my folks."

"Your job at DQ wouldn't be enough to pay all the bills."

Sonja shrugged. "I'll get roommates. I could put a flyer up at school."

"If it was only that easy. I'd love that, I really would, but sometimes it's not in the plan."

"Come on, Ruby. This is your home. It's more than a home, it's a feeling."

"I know. And I'm feeling poor." I laughed. "Come with me. I need to give Ty a tour."

She bounced across the living room. "As long as you let me tell stories of all the trouble we got into here."

"I wouldn't have it any other way." I smiled.

With her big personality, all thoughts of Liam disappeared, and it was nice to be back to normal.

Chapter 25

"Tell me all about yourself, Ty. Do you go to school with Ruby?" Sonja's curls bounced as she washed my windows, already giving up on telling Ty our stories of mischief.

Ty looked over to me while he swept my hardwood floors, and I mouthed, *I'm sorry,* to him. I was sorry for making him clean and for putting up with twenty-questions from Sonja.

Ty mouthed back, *you owe me one*, before answering Sonja. "No, I don't go to school with Ruby. We ran into each other a few times around town, and she borrowed some money from me to do her laundry."

Sonja laughed. "That sounds like Ruby."

Of course, she was referring to pretty much every time we'd had a girl's night out. I never brought enough money along to match Sonja's action-packed evenings. "Hey, you forced me to borrow money. I'd have been completely happy staying home every Friday night."

"With Geoff," Sonja waved me a limp hand. "P-lease. I couldn't get you away from him enough. He stole my best friend away."

"He didn't steal me away," but as Sonja gave me a pathetic look, I realized she was right. I did pass up our time together to hang out with Geoff. What type of girl was I?

"And now, when you're finally free of that loser, you're two hours away from me!"

I laughed. "It's fate."

Sonja moved to another window. "Okay, back to Ty. If

you don't go to school, what do you do for a living?"

He needed to be bailed out. I needed a subject change, but Ty beat me to it. "I work in precious metals." And hunting dragons.

Sonja tilted her head.

"I acquire them then sell them at a higher price."

"Like you flip coins? Like you would flip houses? Get it?" Sonja joked.

We all laughed, and that was the end of that. We spent the rest of the evening dusting everything, washing floors, and rearranging the little furniture I had left to make the house look presentable.

When we were done, Sonja looked at her phone. "It's ten PM already! I gotta run. Dad said I needed to be home already."

I stuck out my pouty lip, and she laughed. "Are you still in town tomorrow? Maybe we could catch a movie?"

I looked to Ty, then back at Sonja. "How about we rent a movie instead? I have a hankering to see *The Princess Bride*. You should bring Ollie, too."

"Oooh, a double date. Sounds great!" Sonja gave me a hug and headed out the door before I could argue about the date comment.

"She's feisty," Ty said. "Carries a lot of personality for being so small."

"She's always been like that. She balances me out some. I can be overly serious sometimes, and she is a beacon of light. She brings out the fun side of me...like...well, you do sometimes." I smiled, thinking about how Ty and I were a good match like Sonja and I were. I locked the door and returned to the living room where Ty stood in front of my piano.

"What is this, exactly?"

I laughed. "You haven't seen a piano before?"

Ty shook his head.

I lifted the fallboard to show the ivory keys. I tapped the middle C.

"Hmm." Ty rubbed the cleft in his chin. "It's like a clavichord."

"A what?"

"Clavichord. Here." Ty sat down beside me and began to push a few keys, filling the air with an unfamiliar melody.

"You play?"

He shrugged. "My parents made me learn when I was younger. Said all proper young men with any bit of money at all knew how to play an instrument." Ty laughed. "Little did they know I'd never be proper, no matter how much they tried. How about you?"

"Many, many years of lessons, but it was my own doing. I love the instrument." My stomach tensed, realizing I hadn't played since mom died. "At least, I used to love the instrument."

"What happened?" Ty asked.

"I—I just don't see a point of playing anymore."

He nudged me with his shoulder. "Come on. I'd like to hear something."

I was going to refuse, but when I looked into Ty's eyes and saw the excitement of a child, I laughed and shook my head. "Okay. Something quick."

He tightened his lips and nodded.

I straightened myself in front of the keys and dug through the songs in my head for something I remembered.

"Okay. Here we go." My fingers struck the keys, first my left hand getting the chords, then adding my right hand. My eyes closed, and I let the melody of *All I ask of you* from *The Phantom of the Opera* fill the room.

I had played this song a million times while practicing for a talent show my freshman year of high school. While I played, the lyrics filled my head, making me remember why I loved the song so much. It was before I had a boyfriend and the song resonated with my idea of the love I hoped for one day— just someone to hold me and be with me. Now, it meant something else. It reminded me of being alone.

A tear pricked my eyes, but I kept them closed, pushing through the song, like if I didn't finish, my world would dissolve into blackness.

Eventually, the song came to an end, and I relaxed. Opening my eyes, Ty's closeness startled me. I had been so carried away in the music that I forgot anyone was in the room.

"You're crying," he said, wiping my tears with his rough thumb.

"I am. I—I just haven't been able to get myself to play since Mom died. It was a bit emotional for me."

He smiled, and the moment was way more melancholy than I would have liked, but Ty came to my rescue. "Well, I have something to play for you."

His fingers clumsily struck the keys, filling the room with a jagged song, but the upbeat melody of it was clear. It only lasted a few measures, then he laughed. "It's a children's song about chasing dragons."

"It was good." Honestly, it was, and it was nice to have music in common with Ty.

He laughed. "No, it wasn't. Like you, I haven't played

since my parents died." Ty sprang up and took my hand, plopping us down on my sofa. "I don't know about you, but I'm exhausted."

"You? You're the one who slept for our entire drive here."

"Hey, hey. You don't have to bring that up. It was a moment of weakness, and it won't happen again. I've been over every inch of this place, and it seems like this is the only place to sleep." Ty fanned his arms out to the sofa. "I call dibs."

I laughed, pushing his legs out of the way and laying on top of him. "I think it's big enough for the both of us."

He brushed my hair off his face and out of my eyes. I thought he was going to kiss me, but instead, he said, "We need a plan of attack. You're a witch, and Liam seems to be mortal, though he has knowledge of magic stones. This should be an easy win for you now that you know what you're up against. I just wish I knew his intentions. I think he might be the key to me finding my way home. If Liam's from my world, maybe he was the one who opened the portal in the first place."

I sat up. "Liam could have opened the portal?" Then things began to click into place. "I kept being drawn to Kirkwood Avenue, and that's where Liam said his apartment was." My jaw hung open. "I bet your portal is inside Liam's place."

Ty looked away. "Yeah, I guess the portal could be there, but only a witch can open a portal, and you said Liam didn't glow with your magic sight...maybe he knows a witch or is working with a witch." He then looked at me. "But even if we find the portal, I can't leave you knowing Liam is still out here. If he's from my world, he needs to return there with me.

We don't know his intentions with you and I can't leave you...vulnerable."

I sucked in my lip. That would mean I was left here with nobody at all. I had known this was coming, and I reminded myself I wasn't all alone. I had Sonja and maybe Luke. I'd make more friends. Ty had been wanting to go home this whole time, and this was as close as we've gotten so far.

I just hadn't expected Liam to turn out to potentially be a bad guy.

"I can do that little switch places trick to take us to Kirkwood Avenue."

Ty shook his head. "I wish it was that easy. But who are you going to switch places with? Maybe Liam, since he already seems to know about magic, but do we even know where he is?"

"Well, then, get in the car, and we'll drive back tonight."

Ty shook his head. "You've been yawning all evening. I can't imagine driving and sleeping are a good idea. And if Liam has ill intentions, how will we fight him? We don't even know what we're up against. He could have one of these stones," Ty pointed to the protection stone around my neck.

"I don't think so. When I used my magic vision, he had nothing." But back on our date at Prego's, he had told me he collected rocks.

Ty ran his hand through his hair and his lips parted to argue, but then he shook his head. "Even if he did have a charmed object, a true witch's powers are stronger than one stone."

"We have the upper hand."

"Not quite," Ty said.

"We do. We know he's not who he appears to be, but he doesn't know that we know that yet. Sure, he knows I'm a little odd about the bracelet, but we have a bargaining chip."

"The bracelet." Ty's eyes lit up. "It cancels magic."

I nodded. "And we know he wants it back. Once we're back in town tomorrow, I'll text him, apologizing and asking to meet him at his house to return the bracelet. While I'm there, I can look for the portal."

"I don't like the idea," Ty's face was stern.

"We don't have any other option right now."

Ty looked away, but eventually set his jaw. "I'm coming along."

"He'll be suspicious of you."

Ty turned back towards me. "Come on. I'm your cousin." He winked. "You can't let me alone. You promised your aunt, remember?"

I lay back onto the sofa and looked around my big, familiar house, realizing how real my situation was. My mom really was gone. I was being cornered by some man who knew I had magic, and I had nobody who'd help me.

Except a boy, Ty, who might want to kill my best dragon friend.

But right now, it didn't matter. I wanted to forget all of that. "We need to go back tomorrow, but tonight, I'd like one night of normalcy in my house." I draped his arm around me and leaned into his chest. He hugged me back.

I wanted one night where I didn't feel alone.

Where I didn't feel like someone was out to get me.

Where I felt safe.

And Ty was perfect for that.

Chapter 26

It felt like I had just drifted off to sleep with my head against Ty's chest, listening to his heartbeat, and my nose filled with his fresh scent when there was a knock at the door.

I tensed and so did Ty beneath me. He leaned over the edge of the sofa and pulled a knife out of his leather messenger bag. I hadn't known he had a weapon, but he was hunting a dragon when he stumbled into my world. Ty pushed me back, keeping me on the sofa while he peered around the wall of the entryway, through the small window on my front door.

"It's Liam," he said.

My heart raced. "Don't open it!"

"Of course, I'm not going to open it, but he already knows you're here. Your car's parked right outside." Ty motioned in the direction of my driveway.

Crap. "He doesn't know what my car looks like." At least, I didn't think he did.

"How'd he know where you lived?" Ty asked.

"I own this house. All it takes is a simple google search."

Ty arched his eyebrows and his forehead scrunched at my reference to technology, but I didn't have time to explain when Liam pounded on the door again.

Maybe he just really wanted his bracelet back and would do it civilly, but as the thumping of his fist against my front door intensified, I doubted that.

What to do? What to do? Did I truly have the upper hand because I was a witch? "Since we think the portal is at Liam's apartment, we need to go there and get Liam to return to his world—if we confirm he's from the other realm." I swallowed. That meant Ty would return too. I shook that thought away. We'd address that later. Now, my focus was on Liam. "If we confirm he's out to get me, and we send him to the other world, is there a way to keep him from returning here?"

Ty nodded. "A witch can close the portal." A witch like me. "But it's not easy. Only strong witches or those willing to drain their powers for the cause can manipulate portals. It takes a lot of magic."

"I'll do whatever it takes."

Ty nodded like he knew that already. "If Liam is truly not magical, it'll buy us some time until he figures out how to open it again." Ty pushed his lips together and looked down at the floor. "I'll follow him through the portal and make sure he doesn't ever figure out a way to open the portal again."

What did he mean? I looked at the wide blade of the knife he held. Yes, he killed dragons. Would he kill a human, too? Judging by the crazy glint in his eye, he might. There was so much I didn't know about Ty.

"Any ideas on how to get him back to his place?" I asked.

Ty shook his head. "I think our best option is to escape and take him by surprise later. We don't even know if the portal is actually there."

I forced my clenched fists open. Ty was right—again. I picked up my backpack, and tossed my keys into the side pocket, draping it over my shoulders, ready to run. Crossing the living room, I stood behind Ty to get a glimpse of Liam. "I need magic sight for a moment. I want to see what we're up against. If Liam has some type of magical object, like the necklace around my neck, I need to know. We can try to sneak out the back door in the kitchen, but he'll notice as we go for my car. We can at least run across the neighbors' yards." But first I needed to get a good view of Liam. I took Ty's hand, seeking comfort in losing my hearing for a moment.

Ty nodded, and I closed my eyes, feeling for my medallion and the necklace around my neck. Liam's pounding abruptly fell to silence, and I opened my eyes to see my glowing arms. I leaned forward to see Liam's continued pounding on the door, and I was glad I did. In his shirt pocket, a light glow pulsated through the fabric.

"Something's in his breast pocket," I whispered. I turned to Ty, and my mouth dried at what I saw behind him. There, across the living room, my mom's old chiming clock still hung on the wall, but somewhere from behind the pendulum, a faint glow filled the room. I tilted my chin and squinted my eyes as I stepped closer to the clock.

Ty caught my hand and turned me towards him. He mouthed, "Ruby, we need to go."

I shook him off, crawling onto the chair beneath the clock and pushing the pendulum aside to feel a deep chamber tucked away in the shadows. My fingers glided across the smooth surface of something inside the clock. I pulled out a shimmering stone, glowing brighter than any other form of magic I had ever seen. I tried to draw my sense of hearing back in exchange for my magic sight, but nothing happened. The rock continued to glow.

Ty tugged me again. We had to go. I hopped down just in time for Ty to jerk his head towards the front door. I caught the swinging panel of wood, and Liam stepping through the opening. The entire scene was terrifying in complete silence. If it hadn't been for Ty here, I wouldn't have even known Liam had broken in without my hearing. My heart hammered and I squeezed Ty's hand so hard, I was surprised he didn't pull away. Instead, he pulled me near.

Do I run?

Was Liam civilized, or was I in trouble?

I mean, he did just break my front door.

I needed to go, but his lips began to move, and I tried to make out some words, but my panic overrode most of my senses.

"Ru-by. You can't hide....bracelet..."

I tugged at Ty's hand and dashed the few feet to my kitchen, heading for the back entrance. Ty stopped and said a few things to Liam, but the men looked like they were going to throw a punch at each other. I turned around and took Ty's hand again, pulling him away. Now wasn't the time for a display of testosterone. If Liam knew about stones and magic, we might not be a match for him.

We made it through the double shutter doors separating the rooms, but before I could reach the exit's doorknob, my legs slowed and it felt like I was walking through honey, then concrete. I couldn't move. I twisted over my shoulder to see a smirk on Liam's lips. "...easy. I need that stone."

Which stone? The one from the clock or the one from the bracelet? I guessed it didn't matter, because I wasn't giving him either one of them.

Ty's face strained as he tried to cross the kitchen to get to me, but we were stuck. Clearly, Liam's doing.

Liam could do magic.

And I needed to do a little magic of my own. A simple switch place spell to put me and Ty in my car would be perfect, but I had nothing to swap places with. As Liam twirled a colorful metal rod with shiny gems molded into the metal through his fingers and stepped through the kitchen entrance, I knew I'd give anything to be out of here right now.

I slipped my hand in my pocket, pulling out both the bracelet and my medallion. I tossed the bracelet on the counter. Sure, I didn't want Liam to get it, but I wanted to get out of here more. The bracelet counteracted my magic—I knew that without a doubt—and I wanted it as far away from me as possible.

Maybe it would even stop whatever magic Liam was doing.

Then, I tightened my grip on my coin and pulled at the magic nestled inside me. Remembering how easy magic had been since Ty had lent me his necklace.

And I cast a spell, wishing Ty, and I were in my car. Not a swap places spell, but a true act of magic that needed a balance. I offered the magic anything it wanted for Ty and me to be safe.

But nothing happened.

I tried again, making bargains with the magic instead of the open-ended one. Make us safe in exchange for my sight…my good grades at school…my mom's house. Anything.

But still, nothing.

It should work. I had Ty's necklace around my neck.

But that necklace should be counteracting Liam's magic, but it wasn't.

What was going on?

Liam was inches from me, and I tried to get away, but the rod he held glowed and my arms froze along with my legs.

My entire body stood rigid. Liam pried my hand open and took the medallion from me, followed by picking up the bracelet on the counter. Right before he stepped away, he tilted his head at me, eyeing the stone I wore around my neck.

Ty jolted his arm, sending something flying towards Liam. I flinched, but opened my eyes to see Liam's body tense. The invisible grip causing me to stand motionless lifted while Liam twisted around, towards Ty, and reached over his shoulder to pull out a knife—Ty's knife—from his deltoid.

We didn't wait around to see what happened next. Ty nearly dove at me, wrapping his arms around my body and pulling me out of the back entrance in one big graceful swoop that clearly would have worked to escape a dragon. Once I righted my feet, I took a sharp corner, dashing through one garage door, and out the front of the house.

As we stumbled into my car, I dug through my bag, pulling out my keys. In no time, I had slammed the car into reverse and backed out of my driveway with Liam standing on my porch. I threw the car into drive and raced out of my neighborhood.

Once I could no longer see my house or the beat-up red car that I assumed was Liam's in the rearview mirror, I glanced over to see Ty's lips moving, but they were so fast, I couldn't determine what he was saying and drive at the same time. I tightened my grip on the wheel. "Ty, I can't hear you, because I still have the magic sight…and my magic isn't working right now to fix it."

After a moment or two, Ty tapped me on the shoulder and I looked over.

"Where are we going?" He mouthed.

I allowed my jaw to relax as I turned back to the road.

"I—I don't know." It was obvious I couldn't fight Liam without my magic. I hoped that the more distance I put between us and that bracelet and him, the better chance for my magic to come back.

All I knew is that I couldn't let Liam keep the bracelet. Whatever that thing had done to me, I didn't need him doing to someone else…if there were other witches here in my world.

And he might not be done with me yet—whatever his plan was.

But that's not what angered me the most.

I was pissed at him for having deceived me.

Pissed at myself for falling for the first handsome face that crossed my path.

I was nothing more than a child, and it was time I grew up.

Chapter 27

My knuckles were white on the steering wheel. I had no idea if Ty was saying anything, but my eyes were focused on the road. He slipped his fingers into my jeans' pocket, and I jumped, but then realized he was fishing for the stone I had pulled from my mother's pendulum clock. Ty slowly pulled the stone out and held it up to the moonlight filtering through the windows, turning it over and making it pulsate in the light. He then dug a box about the size of a deck of cards out of his bag and put the stone inside, wrapping his fingers tightly around the seams.

He didn't say anything for the next half an hour or so, and neither did I. My adrenaline slowly drained, and when I glanced at Ty, he didn't seem tense at all. Perhaps the thrill of dragon hunting made him immune to situations like this. I, on the other hand, was conflicted—wanting to make sure Liam was okay, yet happy we escaped.

Ty appeared more relaxed this car ride. He didn't clench the door handle, but leaned forward with determination in his eyes. Finally, he put his hand on my shoulder, and I glanced over to read his lips. "Try your magic again."

My teeth clenched, but I forced as much calmness as I could muster. "I don't have my medallion."

"You don't need it," He mouthed. "You have this," he touched the pendant laying over my heart. "And this." He tapped my temple.

I nodded, returning my eyes to the road. I pulled at all the magic I could find in me and near me, wishing for my hearing back, in exchange for the magic sight.

I jumped when the sounds of the car filled my ears. After so much time in dead silence, the noise was louder than I expected.

"Are you back?" Ty asked.

I nodded.

He sunk into the passenger seat and rubbed his temple, then leaned over and fingered his necklace I still wore. "My mother told me a story when I was a child about the gem dragons."

"What about them?"

"The gem dragons, like all dragons, have coins as treasure. You have one."

"Had one," I corrected, biting my lower lip, debating if now was the time to tell Ty about Luke, but what Ty had to say now was more important.

Ty nodded. "Okay, had one. But that's not what matters. The dragons also were known to have a second treasure. One that was more valuable and nearly impossible to get because they kept it invisible."

That wasn't hard for me to imagine, as Luke could make himself invisible, so why not his treasure?

"Well, there's a story about a king and queen who were madly in love many years ago…well, at least the queen was madly in love. She discovered her husband loved someone else—a witch who the queen insisted only wanted to take over the kingdom. With each passing day, the queen's suspicion grew stronger until she insisted the witch had her husband under a spell."

"Is that possible? I thought magic couldn't make anyone's will change."

"You do listen to me," Ty teased. "That's not exactly

true. Will can't be changed completely, but a spark can be nurtured and grown. The queen didn't know that. To show everyone that her husband was under a spell, the queen traveled to a neighboring kingdom and sought out the help of another witch. A witch who had a magic stone from the gem dragons. One that absorbed magic."

"Is that what the stone was in Liam's bracelet?"

When Ty nodded, my mind went to another stone I had recently acquired.

"I don't know if this stone," he shook the box in his hand, "and the one in the bracelet are gem dragon stones, but the legend fits. This box blocks magic. I keep it in case I ever need to hide my pendant."

I nodded. "The stones look the same, like an opal. I never held the bracelet up to the moonlight, but I'm certain it's a moonstone, too. Do you think Liam planted it there?"

Ty shook his head. "We left school before he did. I'm not sure."

I swallowed a lump, just thinking about how that stone got into the clock. The car was silent for a bit, but when my thoughts drifted back to Ty's story, I asked, "So, what happened with the king and queen?"

Ty laughed. "The story went that when the queen placed the stone under her husband's mattress, since they had separate chambers, and every time he took the evil witch to bed, more and more of her magic got trapped in the stone, but only no spell was ever lifted from the king. It turned out that he had loved the witch all along."

"That's a terrible story."

"Yeah. It goes on that the queen murdered her husband and the witch was banned from the kingdom forever."

"It's still terrible."

Ty tucked the box containing the stone I had just given him into his bag. "How long had that clock been in your living room?"

"All my life."

He rubbed the stubble on his chin. "And your magic has been weak most of your life?"

"Not weak. It had been non-existent until…" I took a deep breath. "Until I moved out of the house."

"And away from the stone."

My jaw fell open in disbelief. "My mom wouldn't do that to me." She had told me that the clock came from my father. *He* had been the one stopping my magic.

I tensed. He was out to get me from the start—just like Liam.

"Why would Liam want to trap my magic?"

"Because he doesn't have any of his own." Ty's eyes widened, like he just realized something. "Your magic sight confirmed he wasn't a witch, which means, to do magic, he's trapping other witches' magic and using it as his own. Think of it as refilling his stores. A witch makes their own magic, and it's unlimited, for the most part. Big spells use up quite a bit of it and as time passes, the stores refill themselves. Now a regular human, like Liam, can't do magic, but if they have some enchanted object from a witch…I guess it's possible. They would need a store of magic to do spells. And when the magic runs out, they'd have to refill their supply a different way."

My hands hurt from clenching the wheel as we headed down the expressway. "I need to get that stone away from me."

"No, you don't," Ty said. He gripped the leather strap

of his bag tighter. "You need your magic back out of this stone. Eighteen years of magic should be enough to do anything, even close a portal so tightly, nobody can open it again."

* * *

We had a plan and a back-up plan. Ideally, Liam wouldn't be back at his apartment yet, and we'd break in—just like he did to my house—and search for the portal. This plan was great because there wouldn't be a confrontation, but it didn't get my magic medallion back.

We'd use the second plan if Liam was home. His magic came from the wand coated in gems, so we needed to get that out of his hand. Ty said he could handle it, and all I needed to do was distract Liam with an offer of something better.

Like the moonstone that collected eighteen years of my magic.

Nerves caused my palms to sweat as we parked near Kirkwood Avenue. Liam said he lived right above the antique store, but what if he had been lying to me? Now that I didn't hold the magic-sucking moonstone anymore, I tried a simple spell, making my car windows clean in exchange for the dirt to be on my jeans, and it worked. I was ready to face Liam, but I hoped I didn't have to.

Ty was ready, too. He took my hand and led me up the narrow staircase between the antique shop and the second-hand clothing store to a door on top. He hesitated, but I didn't. I pushed the main door open to a narrow hallway with four more entrances leading to different apartments. Which was Liam's?

It appeared it didn't matter. The door to apartment number three swung open, and Liam's tall figure stood beyond the opening. My heart leapt into my throat. The part of me that hoped we were way ahead of Liam on the trip here and would lead us to an empty apartment told me how foolish that thought had been.

I needed my magic vision back. Ty said the portal would glow brightly, but I didn't have a good enough view into Liam's apartment yet to make the necessary sacrifices.

"Ruby," Liam's voice was slick. "You've come to find me." He laughed. "And you brought me that beautiful necklace. And you," Liam's face turned cold as he looked over at Ty, "Where did you get that boot knife? I've never seen one like that in this realm."

Ty ground his teeth together, obviously not willing to answer that question.

"I've come to negotiate," I said.

Liam returned his attention to me and arched an eyebrow. "For the necklace?"

"No. A different stone. One that's been collecting my magic for over eighteen years."

Liam's eyes lit up like a child at an all-you-can-eat candy buffet, but then he squinted at me. "I don't believe you."

I shrugged and stepped back so Ty could show him the stone. Ty pulled it from his bag and slowly slid the cover open, revealing the opalescent moonstone inside. I figuratively crossed my fingers, hoping Liam would take the bait even after Ty lodged his knife into Liam's arm.

"Eighteen years of magic?" Liam rubbed his hands together, but winced when the arm that had been stabbed moved. My eyes focused on the wetness of his black sweatshirt, knowing it was soaked in blood. "That might be all I *ever* need." Ty had been right. All Liam was after was power,

but why? He stepped back. "Well, come in. Let's negotiate."
He pulled the small, pen-like wand from his pocket, and I
tensed.

But what could I do? I wanted to be in his apartment
and had an invitation.

Hesitantly, I stepped over the threshold and sacrificed
my hearing for the magic vision. I was looking for a portal. Ty
tensed, but I pushed forward. Even if Liam ended up with my
magic that was trapped in the stone, what use did I have for it,
anyway? I didn't necessarily want Liam to have it, but if I
could trick him to go through the portal, it'd be worth it. Liam
would be far away from whatever it was he wanted here, and I
didn't need the stone in this world.

I quickly scanned the room for anything that glowed,
but nothing stuck out other than myself, the wand Liam held in
his hand, and something through the fabric of his pocket,
which I assumed were the bracelet and the medallion he had
stolen from me.

Liam leaned against the back of a worn sofa and pulled
the magic items out of his pocket, my eyes confirming he had
what I had expected. He said something, but I missed it. I made
my hearing return and the magic sight disappear. I looked over
to Ty for an inkling of what Liam had just said.

Ty answered whatever question had been spoken.
"We've come to exchange the magic stone for the use of your
portal."

Liam tilted his chin. "Portal?" He laughed. "I haven't
come across a portal in six years. That world is sealed so tight,
nobody can cross. Are you sure you don't want these back?"

He held out my dragon coin and my fingers itched to
grab it, but I wouldn't give Liam what he wanted.

"No deal," I said.

Liam shrugged and dropped the items on a table beside him. "I don't need your permission to get what I want." He twirled the wand between his fingers, and Ty's necklace lifted from my neck. I gripped the pendant with my hand, holding it in place.

"No." Ty ground his teeth, while his hands tightly gripped the little box holding the stone. Liam held out his hand, waiting for the stone and the necklace. In his hand hung the wand, twirling around each finger over and over again.

I looked down and Ty's necklace disappeared from around my neck and appeared right beside Liam on his end table. In my hand was a pencil instead of Ty's stone. Ty's features tensed and contorted as his eyes focused on the necklace that Liam dropped into his breast pocket.

It was time to act. Ty would get the wand and all I needed was a distraction. "Let me show you the stone," I said, taking the box from Ty.

Liam's eyes widened, and I knew this was our opportunity. I stepped close, putting myself between Ty and Liam, yet keeping Liam's focus on the box.

Ty lunged around me, hands outstretched for Liam's wand, but he wasn't quick enough. His body halted in the air, and thumped to the ground.

Now it was my turn. I launched myself at Liam, but toppled to the ground, landing with a thump on top of Ty.

"I never wanted to hurt you, Ruby, but you're not giving me much of a choice," Liam said. "I want your magic. Unlike you, I wasn't born a witch, and I need those stones. I need your power and nobody can get in my way."

From behind me, something scratched at the floor. I

didn't turn around, as I seemed frozen in place again, but Liam's eyes widened and he pushed back into his chair. Luke soared over us and the distraction caused whatever spell Liam had on me to lift. Ty and I stumbled to our feet.

My heart jumped when my dragon dropped down to the ground, standing side-by-side with me. Where had he been? I could have used him earlier. He roared like nothing I had ever heard before—a much bigger sound than his little body should be capable of—and Liam stumbled back.

I took the opportunity to try Liam's own spell on him. Making him feel like he was frozen in concrete in exchange for whatever offers I'd potentially get on my house. Unfortunately, Liam's body still moved, although a bit slower than before. His eyes were still wide at the sight of Luke, and I laughed, but stopped, feeling the massive drain of the magic on me. "Oh, are you afraid of dragons? No need. He's friendly—at least, to me." I couldn't keep up whatever spell I was using to slow Liam down much longer.

Luke flew up, hovering over my head before he dove towards Liam, but swerved when his talons were inches from Liam's shoulder, snatching the bracelet off the table. He then dropped it in my hand. "I can't have this," I said, barely able to keep my eyes open. "It sucks my powers away."

Luke shook his head, taking it from me with his talons and dropping it to the ground. Fire shot from his mouth and smoke rose from his nostrils until the leather strap had turned to ash and the stone glowed red hot. Luke then flew up and grabbed a coffee mug from Liam's end table with his talons and dropped it on the stone. The stone snapped and a fine mist of golden…well, magic, filled the air, circling my body, and clinging to my skin as if I stepped into a cloud of glitter.

My eyes couldn't stop staring at the singed carpet, but as a warm hand took mine, I shook my daze away.

"I suggest we run," Ty said with a grave expression complete with wide, pleading eyes. Did he think I'd stay to fight?

Maybe he was right. I wanted to flee, but my feet stayed firmly in place as an adrenaline like I had never experienced before filled me. A sensation I could only describe as magical.

I tried something new.

I asked my magic for a favor, asking for Ty's necklace back with nothing in return—as a right to balance a wrong.

I held up my hand and wiggled my fingers as the familiar necklace floated out of Liam's pocket and zipped across the room into my hand, feeling exhaustion settle on me stronger than ever, but fighting it off the best I could. The slowness of Liam's body evaporated, and he lunged forward, pointing his wand at us.

Ty didn't give me any more time to make my next move. He practically pushed me out of the apartment, right after Luke. It was clear Ty stepped aside for Luke to pass.

"You saw him," I breathed, knowing whatever spell I had cast on Liam had passed. I struggled to keep up with Ty while my mind was on my dragon. Nobody had ever seen Luke before today, and now, it appeared Luke showed himself to both Ty *and* Liam.

"Your pet dragon?" Ty asked, not giving me a chance to reply. "Yeah. I can see him."

"Are you going to kill him?" The question was heavy on my mind. Killing dragons was what Ty did. I took the final two steps in a hop and sprinted one step behind Ty down the street towards my car.

He called over his shoulder. "Not right now."

My hands balled into fists, and as all three of us—Luke included—piled into my car, I was nearly in tears. "You can't kill Luke. He's my...best friend."

"A dragon?"

When I nodded, Ty threw his seatbelt on and sat back as I maneuvered to get as far away from Liam's place as possible.

The car was completely silent, except for the panting of my little dragon.

My savior.

Ty's savior, too.

I just needed to convince him of that.

Chapter 28

The morning sun blinded my eyes as I drove. When we had a mile or so between Liam's apartment and us, Ty finally drowned out the sound of Luke's heavy breath in my ear. "Where are you going?" he asked.

Where was I going? As I passed a green sign on the highway, saying Arcola was 120 miles away, I knew. "Home."

"It's not safe there. I'm not sure how much magic he has in that wand, but it seems like enough to do some basic spells to locate magic—it's probably how he found you at your school in the first place," Ty said.

"It doesn't matter. It's home, and if Liam will find me no matter where we go, that's better than anywhere else." My fingers tensed on the wheel. Ty was right, and I hated that fact. "Nowhere is safe." I couldn't go to my dorm. I couldn't go home. Where else could I go? A hotel? Maybe by Sonja's place? It didn't matter. "Liam's going to pay." He took my home away from me. He stole my magic. He played with my fragile heart.

And, it appeared, he'd do anything to get Ty and me out of his way.

We drove for a bit more, while all these emotions swirled inside, leaving me with a sense of dread—a sense that I could no longer go on. I couldn't move forward. When my phone rang, and I saw it was the real estate agent, I had to answer. Liam had burst through the door using his magic. I didn't think he broke anything, but she was probably worried about the condition of my house.

"Hello." I answered hesitantly.

"Good news, Ruby!" Her voice was too cheerful, and I cringed. "We're getting an offer on your house."

"Already? The open house isn't until tomorrow."

"They saw the price drop and didn't want to wait. They want to close on it as quickly as possible. Congrats, you'll soon be burden free!"

That's when I lost it.

The pressure. The stress. It all triggered tears. I couldn't talk, much less see the road. Ty took my phone from me. "She'll call you back." He tossed the phone into my console. "Ruby, pull over."

Tears dripped from my eyes. I had nowhere to go. No one to take me in. I might be an adult at eighteen, but I wasn't ready to grow up—at least not as fast as I had been forced to do.

"Pull over," Ty said again, this time with the force of a warrior. I wouldn't argue. I was slowly sinking down a rabbit hole of emotions and driving at seventy-five miles per hour wasn't the wisest.

I wiped my eyes and eased the car off the next ramp and into a gas station's parking lot. I threw the car into park and wiped my eyes again. "I'm okay," I said.

My words were a lie, and Ty saw right through them. He reached over and ran his hand down my back. I didn't want the console between us. I wanted him to hold me while I listened to his heart beat and inhaled his scent.

"We'll get through this," he said.

I let out a sobering laugh. "*We'll* get through this? As soon as *we* find the portal, *you're* gone. Maybe even without Liam. That'd be just my luck."

Ty shook his head. "I won't leave you with him."

Another teary laugh. "You say that now, but when faced with the way home, will you stay?"

"I will. I promise."

"Like my mom promised that it'd always be her and me? How she made plans of visiting me in college? Of being at my wedding. Of babysitting my kids? Or how about my father, that made promises to my mother and couldn't even stick around to see what his child looked like? Who stole my magic for eighteen years?"

Ty tightened his lips, then got out of the car. I had offended him, and at the moment, I didn't care. I watched him walk to the back of the car, and expected him to take off down the sidewalk, but instead, he came around to my side and opened the door. He took me by the arm and pulled me out, and into his chest. His voice was soft. "Ruby, I won't make any promises, but we need to put an end to all this. We need to stop Liam."

I nodded.

Ty and I had the same goal, but what did I expect from him? To give up his home and stay with me, even if the threat of Liam was no more? I hadn't meant to attack Ty, but I also couldn't apologize. I couldn't speak any more about all the people that betrayed me in my life. Instead, I pushed all those memories away and focused on how to send Liam back to his world. "Liam's wand was the only other thing in his apartment that was magical, besides our things."

"Then we need to destroy it."

Luke flew out of the car and rested on the hood. He faced away from us and blew out a breath of dragon fire.

I tilted my chin in question, then remembered the last time he did that. He blew on the bracelet, then it shattered under the weight of a simple ceramic cup.

That was it. "And Luke can help us. Once we destroy his wand, he can't do magic. Without magic, he's no opponent for us."

Ty brushed the hair out of my eyes, and I looked up into his handsome face, waiting for his response. His lips pressed together, then he nodded. "How are we going to destroy it?"

I laughed, nodding towards Luke. "You'll have to ask him."

It was that moment that I went from feeling alone in life to blessed—even if it was just for a moment. I wasn't alone. I had Ty and even when he left me, I'd remember him and feel like I still had a friend out there, somewhere. Knowing Ty for a short time was better than not knowing him at all. I had Sonja back home, and she'd be around for a long time, and I had Luke. Maybe he'd stay and not leave me when we got to the portal.

I took a step away from Ty and began to pace to clear my head. "We just need to find the portal. Liam didn't seem to know where it was, or even believe there was one."

Ty set his jaw. "I don't know if I believe him."

"We have something he wants. I don't know why he'd lie."

"He's the bad guy. That's what they do."

I shook my head. Yes, Liam was the bad guy—or at least he was doing bad things—but I didn't want to believe he had tricked me as much as it appeared. He was a nice guy that made me feel welcome on my first day of school. He gave Geoff something to be jealous about. In fact, he helped me with Geoff in multiple ways. I didn't want to believe it was for no reason other than to steal my magic. There was sincerity to his actions, there had to be, otherwise, I was the biggest idiot in this world...and possibly in Ty's as well.

Ty leaned against my car. "Okay. Let's just say that Liam doesn't know where the portal is. We're back to the beginning."

I looked over at Luke. "Not quite." I squatted in front of my car, bringing me eye-to-eye with my dragon who still sat on the hood. "Ty, you said you chased a dragon through the portal."

"Yeah. That dragon." He pointed at Luke.

"The timelines match. It's about when I started seeing Luke again." I reached out my arm and ran my hand down his head, like how one pets a dog. Luke purred. "Luke, do you know where the portal is?"

Luke shrugged.

I tried again. "Do you remember how you got here, to this world?"

Luke scratched his chin with the tip of his wing, then nodded yes. My stomach did a somersault while Ty squatted beside.

"Luke, can you take me back home?" Ty asked.

Luke nodded and his wings flapped rapidly, lifting him off the roof of the car. He motioned for us to follow him.

I arched an eyebrow at Ty. "Let's go hunt down this portal."

And in a split second, Ty leaned down, planted a peck on my lips, then returned to the passenger side of the car with a huge smile on his face.

He did want to go home, and I understood that feeling. My heart ached, but I pushed it aside. He said he wasn't leaving me yet, and I'd take that bit of comfort for now.

If he did want to go home, there was no way I'd stand in his way. At least Ty had a home to go to.

Mine was about to slip through my fingers.

Chapter 29

We drove through the side roads of Bloomington with a dragon in the lead, flying just beyond my hood. We didn't leave a wake of traffic accidents, so I imagine Luke was keeping himself invisible to everyone except Ty and me.

After about twenty minutes, my eyes whipped to a big blur of something purple and remarkably dragon-like that whizzed by us in the other lane of traffic.

I was overtired. "Did you see that?"

Ty sat up and rubbed his eyes. Had he fallen asleep or was he car sick again? "See what?"

"I thought I saw another dragon."

Ty adjusted his seat to sit up straight. "If we're near the portal, something else could have escaped. You'll have to make sure the portal is closed after I go home, otherwise, your world may get overrun with creatures from my world, and not all of them are as friendly as Luke."

"How am I going to do that?"

Ty pulled out his magical box holding the gem from the clock. "There's eighteen years of magic in this stone. It should be plenty for you to just wish it shut."

My mouth dried, making swallowing impossible. If I closed the portal, whoever was still in this world would be stuck here…like Luke or whatever dragon just flew past us. They'd never be able to return home. "I—I don't know if I can do that. How many creatures, or people like you, are in this world? I can't force them to stay."

"I doubt there are other people here. I only stumbled upon the portal because I was deep in the forests surrounding the gem dragons. And other creatures?" Ty laughed. "I doubt anyone has come, otherwise this world would be in panic."

But I had just seen a purple dragon, hadn't I? If there were creatures here, I needed to gather them up and send them all through the portal before I closed it. Easier said than done. I tapped my finger against the steering wheel. As much as I needed to close the portal, I couldn't. At least, not yet.

"Look familiar?" I asked as we pulled down a driveway lined with evergreens of a nature park on the west side of town.

Ty shook his head. "Our worlds don't line up perfectly which causes portals to move around."

"Then how did Luke know where to go?" I asked.

Ty shrugged. "Dragons can see magic, just like your magic sight. They are also drawn to magic to a degree not even comparable to that of witches. He probably sniffed it out, like a hunting dog sniffs out its prey."

The entrance dead-ended into a parking lot. I was out of breath by the time I cut the engine and maneuvered out of the car, trailing after the dragon through the park. Ty was ahead of me as he hiked down a narrow trail that wound between some deciduous trees, down a few steps to a river. Luke disappeared ahead of us, and I was having a hard time keeping up while avoiding debris laying over the unused trail we were on.

Ty glanced over his shoulder with a large, boyish grin covering his face. "Follow me, Princess. I live for hunting dragons."

I laughed, but then stopped as I realized Ty was one-hundred percent serious.

My legs felt like lead as I struggled to keep up with Ty. He was flying down the trail, gliding over a few trees and rocks like they were only small cracks in the sidewalk. He was good at this. When we got to the stream, he took a giant leap, making it to the other side with a thud.

He turned back to me, but I waved him ahead, pointing to a bridge just up the way. Ty was hesitant, but I didn't wait for him to argue. I headed up the trail and crossed the bridge, excusing myself as I passed a young couple with rosy cheeks and way-too-red lips. I chuckled to myself, not needing any more visual to know what I interrupted.

Out of breath, I stopped underneath a railroad tunnel. Ty lay against the stone structure, looking at a wall across from him. He nodded forward where Luke hovered around the corner in front of a collection of thorny bushes. Ty didn't have to say anything, but I knew what he wanted—my magic sight.

I took a moment to catch my breath, since Ty and Luke had finally stopped their mad romp through the woods. I bet they both enjoyed their early morning exercise, propelled forward for sport rather than the urgency of our situation. If that was the case, they could give me two minutes for my legs to stop burning and my breath to catch.

Ty laughed. "Didn't you enjoy that?"

"No," I shot him a look, but then turned away when I saw his smile. Ty had loved the adventure. Maybe it was best for him to return to where he could be so careless and free. For a moment, I thought of going with him, but stopped that thought immediately. What girl follows someone to an entirely different world after knowing them for two weeks?

And this world was my home. I belonged here. I was in college. I had a house—for the time being. My mom was buried here.

I sucked in my bottom lip and gripped Ty's necklace, pulling out my magic sight.

Right behind Luke was a dark hole filled with a golden shimmer, about eight feet tall and only a few feet wide. It had to be the portal. I did something different, digging deep to my magic and gave Ty the magic sight as well, in exchange for my sense of touch.

I don't know if he said anything, because I couldn't take my eyes off the opening between worlds, wondering what lay beyond the golden sparkles. It wasn't what I expected of a portal. To me, it should have been...well, round. Perhaps like a magic mirror with a frame around a swirling opening. Instead, it was more like the tear in my mom's elephant painting. Even the edges of the opening were a bit jagged.

I glanced at Ty and realized he held my hand, but without my sense of touch, I felt nothing. I wrapped my fingers around his, but I must have squeezed too hard, because he let go. I then took the magic sight away from us both so things could return to normal.

Ty pointed towards the opening that was there, but we could no longer see. "That's not a portal."

My heart raced. "It's not what I was expecting..."

"It's too big. It's not...well, perfectly symmetrical. It's like a rip in the fabric between our worlds."

"I don't understand."

Ty wrapped his arm around my waist and pulled me into his body as we stared in the direction of the opening. "Something different is going on here, and I don't know what it is."

"Will it still take you home?"

Ty let out a sound that combined a grunt with a moan. "I imagine it will, but it's not a portal where magic can just shut it off—" His words fell silent as long, skinny fingers slipped out of…well…the place where I knew the portal was, followed by a head of something that didn't look quite human.

Ty yanked me back and around the corner of the train trestle opposite the portal. Luke zipped beside us, hidden from view. I returned the magic vision to both Ty and me, and we peered out, watching a little man with deep brown skin and pointed ears crawl out of the magical opening between our worlds. While the creature no taller than my knee pushed his way through the opening, its edges ripped bigger. I returned our sight to normal.

"What's that?" I whispered.

"A brownie. They're a bit annoying. You don't want one following you home."

The brownie rubbed his hands on his grey bib overalls, then looked up at the forest canopy. "Let me try to send it back," I whispered, wondering what creature was next. I swear there was a dragon in this world, and now a brownie. How much of Ty's home had come here? How much of our world had gone into Ty's? "I need to stop things from crossing through." I squeezed Ty's jade pendant and dug deep for my magic, urging the creature to crawl back into the hole. I offered the magic my sacrifice of giving up pizza for a year in exchange. Torture, I know, but Ty said to over-deliver on my end of the deal, but nothing happened.

"Why can't I urge him back?" I asked. I knew Ty's pendant was not as powerful as my coin, but it had worked before.

"You can't change free will."

I had known that, but I still expected magic to solve everything—especially with how easy magic came to me at times. I hadn't wanted to close the portal with the potential for things being separated from their home, but after watching the brownie cross, I knew I had to do something before more beings were separated from their homes. I'd figure out how to return things home later. "I need to do something about that opening now." I took a deep breath, not believing what I was going to say. "Ty, you need to go through the portal so I can close it…or at least try to close it."

"Liam's still out there."

"I can handle him. You need to go now. This may be your only chance. Once I close the tear, I'm not sure if I could open it again, and I'm not sure if I should. I'll be fine, I promise."

Ty's laugh broke the downhearted mood. "I may steal for a living, but I don't go back on my promises. We need to get Liam taken care of as quickly as possible, then I'll return home, and you'll fix that tear."

As the brownie took off down the trail, my heart fluttered. There was no more wasting time. We needed to do something—and fast.

I pulled out my phone and sent Liam a text.

Ruby: I want to talk. Meet me at Smithsonian Park on the West side.

Maybe it was foolish to bring him here, but I liked how secluded the park was—besides, I had nowhere else to go.

Chapter 30

For nearly five minutes, I had thought that Liam wouldn't come, but he returned my text with a question.

Liam: What's the catch?
Ruby: I want my medallion back. I'll give you whatever else you want.

Honestly, it was true. If push came to shove, I'd give anything for the coin from my father. It was my only link to where I came from and who I was, plus, I relied on it for my magic to work. It focused me. I told Liam where to find me in the parking lot, and by the time we hiked out of the woods, Liam's beat-up red car was beneath an oak tree, and he leaned against a picnic table, waiting for me. His one hand cupped his upper arm where Ty's knife had cut him during the night, but didn't seem affected by the incident otherwise.

My palms began to sweat, yet I kept Ty's hand in mine. "How'd he get here so quickly?" I whispered.

Ty shrugged. "He must be able to follow your magic."

I swallowed. This confirmed I wasn't safe anywhere. If Liam could do that, how much stronger were his powers than mine? I could sense some magic, like the portal, but nothing strong enough to track Liam down, but then, I only really started to understand this magical world when Ty came into my life. There was so much I still didn't know. I pushed my concerns aside, needing to focus on the plan Ty came up with.

I didn't feel right about his idea, but we were running out of time to put together something better. As Ty disappeared with Luke behind him into the thick bushes of the forest, my heart pounded, and I tried to remind myself of Ty's words. That an out-of-control magic stealer was nothing compared to some dragons he had fought. That we'd be okay.

I didn't believe him, but, as Ty hung back in the woods and I stepped off the trail into the mowed grass, we didn't have much of a choice.

Liam stepped closer, but only so close. We both stopped with multiple car-lengths between us. He must be as untrusting of me as I was of him, but I needed to get him closer to the woods so Ty could wrap his arms around Liam's neck. We thought about using magic, but Ty said his weapon was better. He understood the limits of his body, and I wouldn't argue. I hadn't liked Ty's plan, but while we had been hiking out of the woods, he insisted he could make Liam pass out, as long as I could block his magic.

With Liam knocked out the old-fashioned way, we'd have plenty of time for us to get my medallion back and push Liam back through the tear between our worlds.

Liam's eyes narrowed on something behind me, and he took a step away. "How'd you get a dragon?"

Of course, Luke didn't listen to the plan! He was supposed to stay back with Ty so Liam didn't get suspicious. I still needed to get Liam to the forest and at this rate, he was moving away. "It doesn't matter."

"Yes, it does!" Liam shouted. "And your cousin. Where is he now?"

"Another detail that doesn't matter." I twisted my fingers together behind my back, trying to keep my hands occupied while appearing weak and non-threatening.

"I know he's not from here." Liam laughed. "He's

probably not even your cousin! The knife he stabbed me with…was not from this world."

"He's none of your concern. He doesn't have any magic for you to steal."

"I'm not after his magic." Liam's words were full of passion, but not towards me. Where had the man gone who had kissed me? Given me flowers?

My heart raced as I played the part. I needed to back up against the woods, then use my magic to switch places with Liam. As soon as we had swapped spots, Ty would act. Luke was supposed to hang out in the woods with Ty and not to move until we called his name.

I took one step back, and Liam tilted his chin. I needed distraction. I needed to know where his jewel-encrusted wand was hiding. "Show me the medallion so we can get on with this." Another step back.

Liam reached into his pocket and pulled out my coin. I briefly clicked into magic vision to confirm it was the enchanted one. I also saw the glow from his breast pocket, just like where his wand had been hidden when he was at my house a handful of hours earlier. I returned to normal vision.

Everything was going perfectly, and it appeared he was no longer focused on Luke, wherever he was. One more step back. "What do you want for it?"

"I want the stone you mentioned. The one with all the powers. And I want the charm you wear around your neck."

I lifted Ty's necklace up. "This isn't mine to give."

Liam twitched his finger. "I need everything magical you have. Let me see the stone."

I shook my head. "I don't have it here. I hid it to make sure our negotiations are successful." This was my opportunity.

"Set my coin down on the picnic table over there."

Liam didn't like it, but he walked to the table and set my medallion down.

I wanted to ask him to lay his wand down, too, but I knew he'd never part with it, so I didn't even go there. No sense in making him more suspicious. While Liam dug into his pocket, I maneuvered to the forest's edge until I was close enough to hear Ty's breaths right behind me in the bushes. When a bird called over my shoulder and made me jump, I knew it was Ty's whistle—and my time to act.

I began to prepare, thinking of my magical sacrifice I needed to balance the magic. I wanted Liam captured too much and knew it would take a big sacrifice to make it even. Ty didn't know this, but my plan was to give my enemy exactly what he wanted. The stone that held eighteen years of my magic that I had slid into my pocket, still in its protective box.

With one quick movement, I pulled the stone from my pocket, wrapped my fingers around Ty's necklace, and pulled for my magic from the coin on the picnic table and deep inside, instantly switching places with Liam, but leaving the magical stone in Liam's hand.

As soon as had I reoriented myself, Ty sprang from the forest edge with his arm around Liam's neck. Now, I needed to hold back his magic. Since I had taken the protective box with me when I swapped places, I hoped the bare stone in Liam's hand would do something to counteract his wand, but he wasn't a witch and I couldn't be sure. I focused on Liam's magic, asking for it to come to me and I'd sacrifice my own magic.

Yup, it was the biggest thing I could come up with to sacrifice. It was everything I had.

Ty's bicep flexed around Liam's neck, but Liam's long arms, reached into his pocket, pulling out his wand, and just like that, Ty was pushed backwards by some magical force, all the way across the park.

I twisted back to Liam who stood with the stone in his hand and a big smile on his face.

Our plan failed.

But that meant I still had my magic. To confirm, I reached for my magic sight, but nothing changed. I didn't glow, and neither did the stone or the wand in Liam's hand.

My magic was gone, and Liam still had his.

So much for me having the upper hand.

Chapter 31

Liam stood with the stone containing all my old magic in his hand. He rolled it in his fingers while a slow smile grew on his lips. A smile that said something I didn't expect.

Relief.

Liam flicked his pen-like wand in my direction, causing my coin medallion to fly across the distance between us, stopping right in front of him. The early-morning sun shimmered off the medallion as it turned before him. He flicked his wand again, sending it back to me. "You can have it. I never wanted it. It was never more than a bargaining chip."

Of course. He only wanted my powers. Ty was up and running towards Liam with his teeth barred. Liam simply flicked his wand, causing Ty to freeze like he had in my house.

He must have a compilation of many witches' powers in that single wand, with all the different jewels set in the silver shaft. Was he more powerful than me, a quarter witch?

"Luke!" I yelled. I didn't know what else to do. He had been here before, where was he now? In a moment, maybe two, Liam would take off, and I doubt I'd ever see him again.

The woods were silent.

"Luke! I need you," I called again.

It was enough to have Liam turn around. "I still need to know where the dragon and the hunter over there came from."

Leaves crunched from the woods behind me. My heart lifted. Luke was here. He was our back-up plan, given the task of destroying Liam's wand, any way he could. Did he also know he needed to get the stone out of Liam's hands?

My hope was squashed when the little brownie that had

crawled out of the portal earlier ran out of the woods, Luke flying behind him in a flat-out chase with his teeth chomping, completely distracted from his role in our plan.

Liam tilted his head. "Where did the brownie come from?"

Why did Liam keep asking these questions?

Why did he care?

Unless...Ty said it took lots of magic to open a portal.

Liam said his parents weren't around. Maybe it was more than that. Maybe he did have a family, just not here. Maybe they were separated in two different worlds.

My words were hesitant. "Are you stuck here? In this non-magical world?"

Liam turned towards me. His lips tightened and his eyes filled with sadness. "Yes. For over six years." His hand tightened on the stone, and he held his fist up in the air. "With enough magic, I can open a portal and get back."

Was this what it was all about? All Liam wanted was to return home? "You don't need magic. I know how you can get home."

Liam's eyes narrowed while Ty yelled, "Don't trust him, Ruby!"

I ignored him, waving Liam towards the hiking trail that ran along the river. "Come with me. I'll take you to an opening between the two worlds. I'll help you get home."

If anything, it bought time.

"Ruby, don't!" Ty yelled. "He took your magic!"

I shook my head, urging Liam to follow me. He was separated from his home and would do anything to return there. Even though he threatened to, he hadn't harmed me in any way other than stealing my magic—magic that regenerated itself. If I had any way of being with my mother again, I'd take it. I wasn't self-righteous enough to think I wouldn't have done the same thing as Liam. In fact, I may have been more desperate and out of control.

As I headed towards the woods, with Liam behind me, I turned towards Ty, repeating the words Sonja had told me when I was struggling with Geoff. "Sometimes, forgiveness is the best medicine." But it was more than that. Vengeance and fighting were not always the answers. Sometimes, all it took was forgiveness and trust, but I wasn't certain I trusted Liam. In fact, I knew I didn't, but he deserved to return home as much as I wanted a home for myself. I could at least, forgive him.

Ty gritted his teeth.

"Liam, Ty needs to return home, too. Let him go, and I'll show you how to get home."

Liam waved his wand, and in his eyes, I saw the Liam I had been dating…only he was a bit more broken. More lost.

I headed into the woods with Ty immediately behind me and Liam bringing up the back with his wand in his hand. Right before we arrived at the portal near the train tunnel, I turned around. Ty took a step beside me. "Before I show you the way back home, I need that stone back."

"You can have it if you show me the portal first."

"It looks like we're at an impasse then." I crossed my arms over my chest, but my heart beat wildly. Ty put his hand on the small of my back.

"I'm sorry," Ty whispered.

I felt the blood rush out of my head. Sorry for what? Was he going to betray me?

But the softness in his eyes told me that wasn't it. "I'm

sorry for not trusting your plan."

Liam stepped forward and held out my stone. "Sorry, but I don't quite trust you, but I'm willing to take a chance."

"Well, I don't trust you, either, but need this all to end."

Liam's wand was so close. I could reach out and grab it. A vein pulsed in Ty's temple, telling me he was thinking the same thing. We could get the wand and finish our plan, but it didn't seem as important any more.

I led Liam around the train trestle and pointed into the bushes. "It's back there."

Liam tilted his chin and waved his wand. The tear glowed and came into view, even without my magic sight. "It's not a portal," Liam said. "I've never seen anything like it."

"A tear between realms," Ty said. "Once we're through, you both can try to close it. I know Ruby will try, and I'll make sure you do your part." Ty's eyes were menacing as he glared at Liam, ensuring he got the message.

I shook my head. "I—can't. I don't have magic anymore. I sacrificed it to try to get Liam's wand back at the edge of the woods."

Liam nodded at the stone in my hand. "Eighteen years of magic is cooped up in there?"

I nodded.

"Then, you just need to pull it out."

How?

And why was Liam helping me?

While I was pondering Liam's statement, Luke fluttered over and stopped beside a rock near where I stood. He nodded to the flat surface on top. When he gave me another nod, I knew what to do. I laid my stone on top of the rock and stepped back. Luke fluttered his wings, causing him to rise in the air. He then puckered his dragon lips and doused the magic stone with a hefty amount of fire. The rock heated to a golden red, then orange, then yellow. Luke stopped the fire and the stone slowly changed to black.

"Crack it," Ty said.

I found a little rock beside the boulder and gently tapped the top of the black stone until it shattered like dropping a glass. A golden shimmer leaked out of the stone, then lifted into the air like a fine glitter. It drifted to me and lay upon my skin, making me glow. Making my skin tingle. Making me want to do magic.

I lifted the boulder with my magic, making the beautiful colored leaves turn brown and fall from the tree over us in exchange. A simple act with practically no thinking at all—and no exhaustion that usually followed the use of my magic.

Eighteen years of magic. It was strong. So strong, I knew I didn't need the charm around my neck. I pulled it off. "Ty, this is yours."

He nodded. "It's all I have to remember my mom by."

I shook my head, fisting my coin in my pocket. "It's not all you have. She's in here." I touched his heart, then thought of my own mom...and the house that I was selling. "You might not *need* the necklace to remember her by, but a reminder is still nice to have."

Ty nodded and looked into my eyes. Oh, I wanted to kiss him, but he was leaving. Why make it worse than it already was?

Liam cleared his throat. "Ahem. Well, I see why it didn't quite work out between us—there's no way he's your cousin." He laughed. "Plus, there's the fact that I stole your magic and all."

I glared at him.

"Well, I will be going. I have a family to find." He stopped a second with real sadness in his eyes. "And I hadn't been lying before. My mom really is dead, but I do have a father and two brothers. I'll be waiting on the other side to help close the portal." And that was all I saw of Liam. He turned his back to us and disappeared through the tear, and for some reason, I trusted him to help.

"Maybe I should have taken his magic wand," I said.

Ty shook his head. "He's heading right into a dragon forest. He's going to need it."

We stared at where the opening was for a few minutes more before I spoke what I had been dreading. "It's time for you to go. Liam is waiting to close the portal. I'd hate for him to take off before we get a chance to fix the tear."

Ty wrapped his hands around my waist and pulled me close, doing what I had been avoiding. His lips touched mine and my heart skipped. My hands had a mind of their own as they ran down his chest, then back up, wrapping around his neck and twirling in his hair. There was an untapped connection between Ty and me, which would be lost in a moment's time. He'd step through that portal, and that'd be the end of us.

Everyone left me.

It's how my life was destined to be.

Luke flew up beside us, examining our lips enough that I had to pull away.

"And I suppose you're going back, too." My words were playful, but they didn't cover the sadness I felt.

Luke shook his head way-too-fast, and he dropped

down to my waist, wrapping his little arms around me the best he could. He then dropped to the earth and planted his feet firmly on the ground.

Ty laughed. "It looks like Luke is much smarter than me."

"What do you mean?"

"He's staying here."

I dug deep. There was something I wanted to say, and I didn't know how Ty would react. What did it matter? If he said no, I'd never see him again, anyway.

I cleared my throat. "You—you could stay." As I said the words, tears rushed to my eyes. Hadn't I already admitted to myself I couldn't leave my home for him. How could he leave his for me?

Ty tilted his chin, and I looked away, trying to hide my emotions. He noticed them anyway. He lifted his hands and wiped my tears with his thumbs. "I don't belong here. Everything I know is back there. That world is my home."

I nodded. I completely understood.

Ty kissed me again, and I pulled away.

"Let's not make this harder than it needs to be," I said. "Go. Thank you for all you did for me."

Ty's lips tightened, and he shook his head. "No, thank you. You did everything for me."

My tears burst through like water over a dam while Ty turned back to the opening. He crawled into the bushes, but before he left, he turned my way and blew me a kiss. "Give me a minute before trying to close the portal."

I nodded, but before Ty turned back towards the opening, I saw his lip quiver. He was going to cry, too.

That big, strong dragon hunter was going to cry.

Before I could croak out another plea for him to stay, he stepped inside and was swallowed up by the rip between worlds.

And here I was.

Alone.

Well, not quite alone.

I had my dragon best friend.

And a little bit of hope filled my heart.

Chapter 32

Luke flew over to the portal and looked inside, then pulled back. He spun around in a circle and flopped on his back in the middle of the trail. He wiped his arm across his forehead and blew out a puff of smoke.

I laughed a tear-filled laugh. I was that exhausted, too.

I waited nearly a minute, then pulled for my magic. Here we go. Sealing the hole. Kissing Ty goodbye…in a figurative sense.

I didn't need an exchange to make my magic work, losing Ty was enough of a sacrifice. In fact, I'd say magic owed me one. I focused on the portal, aiming my magic towards the start of the rip, like I had with my mom's painting, and began to imagine it closed. As I put all my energy on it, nothing happened.

Except a voice from the other side.

"Wait!"

It was Ty. I halted as Ty crawled out of the opening. "I remembered something you said to Sonja."

I tilted my head. My emotions were swirling, and I couldn't think straight.

Ty crawled out of the bushes and stood before me. My tears were coming again. It would have been easier if he had stayed on the other side.

"What did I say?"

Ty smoothed the hair out of my face. "You said home wasn't a place, it was a feeling."

I nodded. "I meant that it wasn't the house I loved; it was the memories of Mom."

Ty nodded. "That world back there, it isn't home. My family is long gone, and I have nobody…but I have someone here. Why would I leave you behind?"

"Because we've only known each other a few weeks."

"Ruby, that doesn't matter. We have a bond."

And I felt it too. "Are you staying with me?"

He nodded.

"Are you going to kill my dragon?" I asked with a tear-filled laugh.

"Of course not." Ty laughed and pulled me into his chest.

Home was a feeling. At that moment, I understood that sentence differently. Home was here, in Ty's arms, even if I had no idea where it would take me.

Ty nodded towards the tear between our worlds. "Okay close it before anything else escapes. Liam's ready."

I turned back to the opening. The sooner it was closed, the sooner I'd be certain Ty wouldn't change his mind. I focused on the tear and forced it to be stitched up…in exchange for…the offer on my house falling through. For the financial burden of being a college student trying to care for a house that I could never live in.

Only, the more magic I put into the rip, the more the hole seemed to expand.

"It's not working," I said. "It's growing."

Ty moved forward, examining the opening. He leaned inside and disappeared.

Dang it. I didn't get it closed in time. I wrung my hands together, waiting. Each breath was like an eternity, hoping Ty would return.

He would. He promised me.

Luke circled at my feet.

"He'll be back," I assured nobody except myself.

When Ty crawled out of the tear, butterflies filled my stomach and a huge black cloud blew away.

"Liam's sealing the inside with magic. It won't close the portal, but it'll stop critters from accidentally crawling through into *our* world. He said he'll find a master witch to fix it."

"So, we're just supposed to walk away?" It didn't seem right.

Ty draped his arm over my shoulder and nodded. "Yeah. Sometimes, there's nothing more you can do."

"And we trust Liam?"

Ty nodded. "He put the spell on it already. I tried to crawl through but was blocked."

I took a deep breath. "Why did the hole grow when I tried to close it?"

Ty shrugged. "Why are you full of all these questions? Instead, you should focus on taking me home."

Home. Yes, an image of that Victorian home flashed through my mind, but I stifled it out, replacing it with my tiny dorm. Ty couldn't stay there.

I sucked in my bottom lip, the thoughts of staying here in Bloomington churned my stomach. I had nothing here. Sure, Ty and Luke would be wherever I went, but home was that Victorian house.

"We're going to Arcola."

"But you have school."

"I'll transfer. There's no reason why I'm in Bloomington, anymore. It's just costing me more money to be away. In the past month, I learned from Liam, trying so

217

desperately to return home, Kat, a girl I only knew for a week, and you," I gave Ty a quick peck on the cheek, "that if things don't work for you, change them. And I'm one-hundred percent certain Bloomington doesn't work for me. Not that city. Not that school. Not Geoff. I just hope Sonja was serious about wanting to move out. I could use the income from renting out a room."

Ty lazily walked me back to the parking lot. "That house is big enough for more than Sonja. Don't you have four bedrooms? I'm sure you could even get another roommate or two."

I nodded. It would feel nice to have some life back into that empty home. "I was hoping you'd be one of them."

Ty's voice grew soft. "I was hoping I'd get to stay in your room." He chuckled as he leaned down and kissed me, but I playfully pushed him away.

"You did, huh?"

"I mean, don't I deserve it? I gave up my entire world for you."

"Oh, come on. You knew the tear wouldn't close."

Ty just laughed. "And you need me, anyway. That patch Liam put on may not hold. Who knows who'll be next to try to steal your magic?"

"And of course, a dragon hunter in this world may be good. I know there is at least one purple dragon out on the run. And I could use someone to help me with my house. It's in desperate need of a bit of maintenance. The front door might even be broken."

"Well, it looks like this is only the start of our adventure."

And it was. Not an end, but a beginning.

And I had someone to share that journey with again.
It was a happy thought that I didn't ever want to let go.

MAKE SURE YOU CONTINUE RUBY & TY'S
ADVENTURE WITH BOOK 2 IN THE **QUARTER WITCH
CHRONICLES**, **_WHILE THE DRAGON'S AWAY_**.

Thank you for reading _Dragons are a Girl's Best Friend._
Make sure you read a sneak peek of book 2, _While the
Dragon's Away_ **at the end of this novel.**

If you'd like to be notified when I have new books available
or am running sales on my current library, please subscribe
to my monthly newsletter here:
www.JoynellSchultz.com/Subscribe. At times, I give away
free stories, so if you loved this book, you'll want to make
sure you receive my newsletter.

Don't forget to leave a review. Feedback from readers like
you help authors and readers come together. You can leave
a review on Amazon here.

And finally, I try to make my books as error-free as
possible. If you caught a type-o or other inconsistency,
please email me at joynells@gmail.com so I can update this
manuscript for other readers.

Other Books by Joynell Schultz
<u>(View entire collection on Amazon here)</u>

-- QUARTER WITCH CHRONICLES –
Not every witch has a pet dragon.

<u>Dragons are a Girl's Best Friend</u> (Book 1)
<u>While the Dragon's Away</u> (Book 2)
<u>A Good Dragon is Hard to Find</u> (Book 3)

-- ANGELS OF SOJOURN --
These angels don't have halos.

<u>Blood & Holy Water</u> (Book 1)
<u>Fangs & Fairy Dust</u> (Novella – Optional Book 1.25)
<u>Bitten</u> (Short Story – Book 1.75 & free to newsletter subscribers)
<u>Fur & Feathers</u> (Book 2)
<u>Flame & Fortune</u> (Stand-alone Novella & Optional Book 2.5)
<u>Souls & Shadows</u> (Book 3)
<u>Broken & Burnt</u> (Stand-alone Novella)
<u>One Possible Future</u> (Stand-alone Short Story)

-- TALES OF THE FAIRY GODMOTHERS --
A magical pregnancy to a long-lost childhood love, meet your fairy godmother.

<u>Hidden: A Pregnant Fairy Godmother's Journey…</u>
<u>Trapped: One Fairy Godmother's Impossible Love…</u>

-- SWEET LITTLE HOLIDAY ROMANCE --
Need the perfect man? No problem. Simply create him!

Created for Christmas
Validated by Valentine's
Hitched on Halloween (Coming 2019/2020)

Built for the Billionaire: A Sweet Little Dystopian Romance
(Coming 2019)

-- THE SUPERHERO WIVES WORLD --
Find out what happens after the superhero gets the girl.

The Secret Lives of Superhero Wives
The Superhero's Husband
The Superheroes' Wives World (Collection of 3 short stories
free for newsletter subscribers.)

-- EARTH'S ONLY HOPE --
Another ice age is coming, and an alien race offers salvation.

Connecting (Prequel Coming September 2019)
Departing (Book 1 Coming September 2019)
Surviving (Book 2 Coming Fall/Winter 2019)
Returning (Book 3 Coming Fall/Winter 2019/2020)

-- STAND-ALONE NOVELS --
Love, Lies & Clones: A Futuristic Mystery Novel

About the Author

Joynell Schultz was raised at a zoo (yeah, bring on the jokes) which gave her a love of animals. She's a pharmacist by training, but spends her days working at the family-owned zoo and spends her nights (cough, cough—very early mornings) creating imaginary worlds writing speculative fiction.

When she's not trying to put food on the table (takeout, of course) for her husband and two children (and keeping it away from her sneaky Great Dane), she spends her time reading, writing, enjoying the outdoors, and planning her next vacation.

Contact Info:
Email: joynells@gmail.com
Facebook: http://www.facebook.com/joynelljschultz
BookBub: https://www.bookbub.com/authors/joynell-schultz
Blog: http://www.joynellschultz.com

Stay informed of new releases, news on books in progress, and exclusive content delivered to your email inbox once or twice monthly by subscribing to *Joynell's Hidden Worlds Newsletter*.

Sign up here: http://www.joynellschultz.com/subscribe
You'll receive two free eBook collections in the first email!

Chapter 1: While the Dragon's Away

"Do you think there really is a dragon?" Sonja twirled a blond curl between her finger in front of the TV. Her books were laid out on her lap, but I could tell she wasn't really studying.

After a full day of college—filled with normal things like chemistry, calculus, and English literature, the question from my best *human* friend, and roommate, wasn't what I expected.

My mouth dried, and I closed the old wooden front door of my Victorian home. I took off my backpack and draped it over the chair beside where Sonja sat with her legs tucked beneath her. Had she run into my invisible friend, Luke? Did he blow a breath of dragon fire and set off the smoke alarms? Or, had Ty told her something about the magical realm he came from?

I played innocent. "What do you mean?" I leaned on the back of the chair and tried to look as nonchalant as possible for someone hiding a secret.

Sonja motioned towards the TV, bouncing a bit on my sofa. "The news keeps reporting about a seven-car pileup over in Terre Haute and two of the victims swear they saw a dragon."

"That's ridiculous," I huffed, grateful I had taken that acting class in high school. If only Sonja knew she shared a house with a dragon, a witch, and a man from another world.

Ty entered the room through the shuttered door hanging between the living room and kitchen. I'd never get used to how domestic he looked holding a hammer and wearing flannel PJ pants and a white t-shirt that did nothing to hide his broad chest. "Did someone say dragon?" Once a dragon hunter, always a dragon hunter. Sure, it was nice not having to struggle to find his green eyes, but he looked a lot less like trouble and more like the nice boy next door. Although to be honest, I guess he was a bit of both.

"Ignore that and get dressed. I'm surprised you're not ready." I glanced at the time on my phone. "We have someone coming to see the house in fifteen minutes."

Ty set the hammer down on an end table and looked down at his plaid PJ pants. "What? These are the most comfortable pants I've ever worn. Is there a rule I can't wear them in public?"

"Yes."

"Not if you're going to Walmart," Sonja joked. I couldn't help but nod my agreement. She got me on that one. Sonja pointed her pencil towards the TV. "Check out the news report. These two people swear a dragon caused their car crash."

Ty jumped over the side of the sofa and sat beside Sonja. "No fooling." He laughed. "This is so much more fun than fixing the cabinet doors." I could see the glint of excitement in his eye. A glint of…purpose. I hadn't seen him like this since a few months ago when Liam, a man from Ty's magical world (and my ex-boyfriend) stole my magic. Ty and I grew close while scheming a plan to get it back.

Luke fluttered down the stairs. His little wings didn't seem big enough to support the weight of his plump, golden body, but he flew—just like a forty-pound bumble bee. Perhaps my dragon's flight was as magic as whatever kept him invisible to Sonja, but not to Ty and me. Luke tilted his head and looked at me with big red, puppy-dog eyes.

"I really doubt a dragon is running around in Terre Haute," I lied. Don't judge me. Sure, Sonja was my best friend, but she didn't need the complications my magic brought to our lives. She struggled enough focusing on her job at DQ, her boyfriend Ollie, college, and keeping her overprotective parents happy. Truth was, there *might be* a dragon in Terre Haute. Months ago, during my little confrontation with my ex, I swore I saw a big purple dragon go buzzing by my car window. At the time, there was a huge gaping hole between this world and the magical one Ty comes from that anything could (and did) escape.

But what could we do about the dragon?

Liam patched the tear between our worlds after we sent him home. Ty and I had confirmed it. If we went after and actually caught the dragon, we couldn't risk opening the tear up and letting another creature escape while returning it to Ty's realm. Ty's solution would be easy—he'd want to kill the beast. He was a dragon hunter, after all.

The doorbell interrupted our conversation. I circled the sofa and put my hand on Ty's shoulders, giving him a soft massage. "Come on. Put some real pants on." I leaned down and whispered in his ear. "Besides, jeans make your butt look good."

He laughed, but hopped back over the couch and flew up the stairs, two-by-two. It was hard to believe he had passed on returning home to his world to stay here with me. Honestly, I was flattered a little science nerd like me could land such a funny, sweet, and attractive man. Ty was so out of my league, but I wasn't complaining.

Sonja flipped off the TV, and we headed to the large,

wooden entry door. I tried to see out the sidelight and get a good look at our potential new roommate, but all I saw was brown grass and the leafless maple in my front yard. "Here we go. Fingers' crossed." I opened the door.

My heart sank when I saw who greeted us. I knew you shouldn't judge a book by its cover, but the man who stood outside wasn't what I expected. After Sonja and I hung flyers all around campus, I had expected a college student, but this man was more of a college professor.

A retired professor.

I smiled. "Maxwell Smith?"

He nodded. "I'm here about the room you have for rent."

I stepped aside and welcomed him into my house. Behind him, he dragged a small wheelie-cart with a fluffy dog about the right size to dip into a bucket of water and scrub your car with kind of small. Don't get me wrong. I liked dogs—but I was more of a dragon kind of girl.

The dog happily panted as it crossed the threshold, but as soon as its eyes latched on to the chair Luke sat in, the canine's tongue disappeared and a low growl filled the room. Its eyes never left where Luke was sitting. Maybe Luke couldn't stay invisible to dogs.

I raised my voice. "Let me show you around."

The elderly man nodded, and I showed him the large living room and the kitchen with the giant island in the middle. He didn't say anything, but his dog continued to growl and bark.

"All the bedrooms are upstairs. There are three on the second floor and one on the third." I motioned to the staircase. "I'll show you which one would be yours."

The man looked up the stairs, then pulled his dog closer, squatting down to open the cage.

"Wait! You can't let the dog out." My eyes darted to Luke. I nodded for him to head upstairs into my bedroom. Ty stood at the top of the steps and noticed my movements. He followed Luke and shut my bedroom door. Phew. One disaster avoided.

Maxwell proceeded to open the carrying case. "Poochy needs to see the house. She's making this decision as much as I am."

My shoulders tensed and my jaw clenched, but I gave Maxwell an approving nod. Out dashed Poochy, up the stairs, and barking in front of my bedroom door. Oh, sharing a house these two would be a nightmare, but I was running out of choices. Over the months we had been looking for a roommate, we hadn't had a candidate that all three of us liked and who was willing to live this far off campus. We decided to be less picky the past few weeks, since I had bills piling up.

Sonja paid a fair portion for her room, Ty was looking for a job, but it was hard when you didn't have any papers that said you were born in this country, much less this world, and I was slowly running out of the money that my mom had left me when she passed away. Between the house and college, I remembered why I had been trying to sell this monstrosity.

But it would all be okay as soon as we landed a roommate.

The man held tightly to the railing as he inched his way up the stairs, appearing to favor one knee. My stomach turned. He'd turn it down. With the amount of work it was taking him to get to his room, there was no way the house would meet his needs.

At the top of the stairs, I opened the bedroom door that Maxwell would have. It would easily fit a queen size bed, a desk, dresser, and a few more pieces of furniture. Maxwell walked around the empty space. Poochy finally gave up on my bedroom door and joined her owner inside the room.

Only to squat and leave a puddle beneath her on my maple floors.

"Awahw!" I spun around and headed to the bathroom for a roll of paper towel. Maxwell didn't even seem to notice. He just pushed his glasses up and stared out the bay window overlooking the street. Sonja snickered from the hallway.

"It's perfect," Maxwell said. "I'll take it."

My stomach twisted, but I thought of the pile of bills on the kitchen counter, again. He wouldn't stay long. There was no way he'd do those steps multiple times per day, but a month or two of rent, plus a security deposit would go far to catch us up on the water bill.

"Great!" I said. "When will you be moving in?"

Sonja elbowed me. "Actually, we need to talk about it first. We'll call you."

Maxwell nodded and began his descent down the stairs. Poochy had found my bedroom door again and was exercising her vocal cords while scratching at the wood. She was going to destroy this place, and she had only been here for minutes. What kind of damage would she do in a month?

As soon as Maxwell pulled out of my driveway, Sonja shook both her head and her finger at me. "I don't think so."

"We have bills. We don't have a choice."

She laughed. "The dog peed on your floor and wouldn't stop barking. How would we study?"

Ty joined us downstairs with Luke hopping the steps

behind him. "She's right."

My tension peaked in my shoulders, and I rolled it out. "Of course, she's right." I dropped down in the chair and looked to Ty. A few months ago, having us all live together in this house sounded great, and it was great. We were so close to making things work. Who knew finding a roommate would be so difficult? "We'll keep looking."

Sonja headed into the kitchen, leaving Ty, Luke, and me alone.

Ty rubbed my shoulders. He leaned down and whispered in my ears. "We could always hunt down that dragon. Maybe there's a treasure."

I laughed, but he was serious. It's the way he had earned his money back home.

I patted his hand. "Nah, it'll be okay. Maybe it's time I added a job to my list of duties." Though, trying to maintain the house, keep up with school, and keep the man who gave up his entire world for me happy was enough for me to manage, but many people also had a job. I could do it. "We'll get through this month and worry about next month when it comes."

Ty's words were soft, obviously keeping them from Sonja one room over. "Come on, princess. I assure you that dragon hunting's very lucrative."

"So is robbing a bank, but we're not to that point yet."

"We're not?" He arched an eyebrow at me.

"No. Things can still get much, much worse."

"Like having a dragon running around causing car crashes."

"Fine," I said. "If there's any more trouble, we'll check it out."

He planted a soft peck on my cheek that made my heart flutter. "I knew I could count on you."

Now, if only I believed my own words. When it came down to it, I was still terrified of Ty's world, and it was completely hypocritical of me. I was afraid of magic *and* dragons, even though I was a quarter witch myself with a pet dragon who curled up at my feet at night.

What bothered me was that Ty had told me stories of evil witches and curses that existed in his world. I had seen the scars from dragon battles all over Ty's body. I had heard about the curse that had killed his entire family. I had faced Liam, an ordinary human with magical stones that could siphon all my magic away, leaving me completely unprotected. If he could do that, what could a real witch do?

Terrified was an understatement.

Read the rest of Book 2 in the *Quarter Witch Chronicles*, ***While the Dragon's Away*** available through Amazon.

Printed in Poland
by Amazon Fulfillment
Poland Sp. z o.o., Wrocław

51234073R00136